The Girl I Saved on the Train Turned Out to Be My Childhood Friend

Kennoji

Illustration by Fly

©Fly

"Guess we all got caught up in the moment."

Name: Hina Fushimi

Age: 17

School year: high school, second year

Height: 5'3"

Ryou's childhood friend and an immensely popular, gorgeous girl. She started approaching him more aggressively after he saved her on the train.

"So...how did this happen again?"

Name: Ryou Takamori

Age: 17

School year: high school, second year

Height: 5'9"

Self-proclaimed boring dude struggling to fit in. He's recently been taking notice of his childhood friend's...approaches?

©Fly

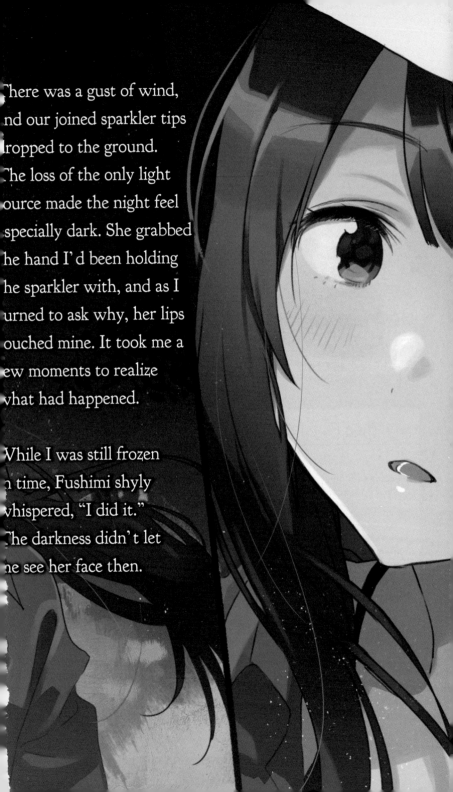

There was a gust of wind, and our joined sparkler tips dropped to the ground. The loss of the only light source made the night feel especially dark. She grabbed the hand I'd been holding the sparkler with, and as I turned to ask why, her lips touched mine. It took me a few moments to realize what had happened.

While I was still frozen in time, Fushimi shyly whispered, "I did it." The darkness didn't let me see her face then.

"Hey, I didn't know we'd end up in the water!"

Name: **Mana Takamori**

Age: 15

School year: middle school, third year

Height: 5'5"

A *gyaru* kind of girl who cares deeply about her brother. She might not look the part, but she's responsible for all cooking and chores in the Takamori home.

"Mana was all like, 'You should sumo wrestle!'"

"I'm soaked, but that was fun."

Name: **Minami Shinohara**

Age: 16

School year: high school, second year

Height: 5'6"

Former classmate of Ryou and Hina's from middle school. She dated him for three days when they were in third year.

Name: **Shizuka Torigoe**

Age: 17

School year: high school, second year

Height: 4'10"

Ryou's lunchtime friend and classmate. She asked him out and got rejected, but it seems her feelings haven't faded away...?

©Fly

The Girl I Saved on the Train Turned Out to Be My Childhood Friend

2

Kennoji

Illustration by Fly

YEN ON

New York

The Girl I Saved on the Train Turned Out to Be My Childhood Friend 2

Kennoji

Translation by Sergio Avila
Cover art by Fly

CHIKAN SARESOU NI NATTEIRU S-KYU BISHOUJO WO TASUKETARA TONARI NO SEKI NO OSANANAJIMI DATTA volume 2
Copyright © 2020 Kennoji
Illustrations copyright © 2020 Fly
All rights reserved.
Original Japanese edition published in 2020 by SB Creative Corp.
This English edition is published by arrangement with SB Creative Corp., Tokyo in care of Tuttle-Mori Agency, Inc., Tokyo.

English translation © 2022 by Yen Press, LLC

Yen On
150 West 30th Street, 19th Floor
New York, NY 10001

Visit us at yenpress.com ✧ facebook.com/yenpress ✧ twitter.com/yenpress ✧ yenpress.tumblr.com ✧ instagram.com/yenpress

First Yen On Edition: May 2022

Yen On is an imprint of Yen Press, LLC.
The Yen On name and logo are trademarks of Yen Press, LLC.

Library of Congress Cataloging-in-Publication Data
Names: Kennoji, author. | Fly, 1963– illustrator. | Avila, Sergio, translator.
Title: The girl I saved on the train turned out to be my childhood friend / Kennoji ; illustration by Fly ; translation by Sergio Avila.
Other titles: Chikan saresou ni natteiru s-kyu bishoujo wo tasuketara tonari no seki no osananajimi datta. English
Description: First Yen On edition. | New York, NY : Yen On, 2021–
Identifiers: LCCN 2021039082 | ISBN 9781975336998 (v. 1 ; pbk.) | ISBN 9781975337018 (v. 2 ; pbk.) | ISBN 9781975337032 (v. 3 ; pbk.)
Subjects: CYAC: Love—Fiction. | LCGFT: Light novels.
Classification: LCC PZ7.1.K507 Gi 2021 | DDC [Fic]—dc23
LC record available at https://lccn.loc.gov/2021039082

ISBNs: 978-1-9753-3701-8 (paperback)
       978-1-9753-3702-5 (ebook)

10 9 8 7 6 5 4 3 2 1

LSC-C

Printed in the United States of America

My shopping bag was heavy with three bottles: oolong tea, orange juice, and cola.

It was still April, and yet the sun was already summer bright; the UV rays were like needles on my skin.

Fushimi was walking ahead of me, basket in hand.

"Can't we just sit around here already?" I called.

"There's a better place up ahead."

We were at an open green area of the park.

"C'mon, hurry!" Fushimi cheerily urged me on.

I'd known Fushimi since preschool, and she was prettier than any girl I'd ever met. We'd drifted apart during middle school, but recent events had restored our relationship.

Despite her usual atrocious fashion sense, she was actually put together today.

Fushimi hadn't realized the time for cherry blossom viewing had passed when she made the suggestion, so we had to make do with a regular old picnic.

There were groups of people sitting on picnic blankets all around, including families and college students enjoying themselves in the shade.

"So, how long is Hina planning on having us keep walking?" Mana, my sister, asked me with clear frustration on her face.

"Don't ask me."

Mana was holding our lunch box. You couldn't tell from her heavy *gyaru* makeup and street fashion, but she was a responsible girl and a great cook.

"Fushimi looks like she's having fun," Torigoe said, picnic blanket in her arms.

Torigoe was the class librarian and a quiet type. I spent my first year of high school having lunch with her in the physics room, and for whatever reason, she asked me out not long ago.

"Hinaaa? Wait!" Mana ran up to her.

Torigoe and I watched them go.

"You don't mind my sister acting like that? Not exactly a great first impression she's making."

"Nah, I don't mind her."

Huh. That's unexpected.

Mana and Torigoe seemed like polar opposites, but at least there was no conflict brewing between them.

This picnic had originally been planned for Fushimi and me, but then we ended up inviting Torigoe in front of Mana, who also asked to come.

"Ryouuu! Torigoeee! Come quick!" Fushimi waved enthusiastically from next to a big tree.

"Let's go, then."

"Sure."

Torigoe and I walked up to the shade.

"Thanks for inviting me today," Torigoe said.

"You're welcome."

We get to do so much more when two of my friends become friends with each other as well. The circle of fun expands. To be quite honest, I hadn't expected her to come.

"Fushimi seems to want to be friends with you, and I'd like that, too."

I didn't explicitly turn her down when she asked me out, but she had figured out my feelings anyway. Technically, Fushimi was her rival in love. I thought she wouldn't like hanging out with her and me both.

"So the princess wants her own personal, trusty maid."

"I doubt she sees you as a maid."

Fushimi and Mana had been friends for a long time, but they weren't the same age. In that sense, she had better chances of speaking freely with Torigoe.

"I like both of you, so I'm having fun."

"D-don't say it like that. How embarrassing."

"Hey! Don't make it awkward… I tried so hard to play it cool, too." We looked away from each other, then giggled.

"Hina, don't you think Bubby's a wee bit too close to Tori?"

"N-no, he's not. I'm much closer to him anyway."

"Hee-hee, you're jealous."

"No, I'm not."

We reached the pair goofing off and placed the picnic blanket. Finally, *finally* we could sit down.

"Bubby, get the cola."

"Before lunch?"

"Don't judge—just give it to me."

I ceded and poured the cola into a paper cup, then gave it to her. She gulped it all.

"Slow down."

"This stuff is so good. I can feel my max HP going up already."

I kinda get it but kinda not.

Suddenly, I became a drink dispenser, doing all the pouring for everyone.

Fushimi and Mana opened up the lunch boxes each of them had made. Mana's was a classical picnic bento: rice balls, deep-fried chicken, sausage, fried eggs, and potato salad.

Yeah, I saw her cooking this morning, my motherly gyaru *sister.*

"Your sister went for a pretty orthodox lunch, but that's what's good about it."

"Right? You know what's up, Tori."

Mana nodded in satisfaction while glancing at Fushimi's box. It was a field of brown pumpkin.

"Hina… This, um… Is this a joke?"

"Huh? Why? It's good stuff—trust me."

"No, I'm not talking about how it tastes, really…"

There it is again… The leftover bento.

"Oh look, Bubby's favorite. Was this your clever plan all along? Or are you just clueless?" Mana was panicked.

"I—I can't cook anything else, okay? I couldn't risk bringing hot garbage to our picnic."

"Hot garbage…"

"Hot garbage …"

"Hot garbage …"

The other two echoed my reaction.

Mana poked at the pumpkin like a cautious cat, then fearfully took a bite.

"…It's yummy. Not sure what to think."

Having gone through this before, I knew exactly how Mana felt.

"So she couldn't stop herself from cooking a buncha pumpkin while thinking of Bubby."

"Fushimi…are you, like, okay?" Torigoe asked with striking bluntness.

Can't you be a bit more considerate?

Mana was cackling. "Bubby, stop it. Don't flirt with Tori or you'll get stabbed."

"I won't stab him."

"And I'm not flirting." I defended myself.

I was already expecting this to happen, which was why I'd told Fushimi not to bother making lunch, but then she couldn't stop herself from competing against Mana. And everyone ended up making fun of her pumpkin field, obviously.

Each of us got our own pair of chopsticks and plate, and we started eating.

"Your rice balls are so tiny and cute, sis."

"Y-you think? Maybe it's because my hands are small."

Mana blushed, unable to react to the unusual praise. Guess that never occurred to her before.

Fushimi was also waiting excitedly for a review.

I mean, I already ate this not too long ago… But I was grateful she'd made anything at all, so I took a bite.

"Good stuff."

"Glad to hear it." She smiled with the intensity of the spring sun. "Go on, have more."

She pushed her lunch box toward me.

"You can make boiled pumpkin fine, so I'm pretty sure you should be able to handle other boiled stuff…," Mana said, confused as to why it was only this.

"Really, this is the only thing I've ever been able to cook. I screw up everything else." Fushimi smiled awkwardly.

Torigoe took a bite. "Well, this tastes like something an old, retired lady would cook."

"Pffft." Mana almost spit out her cola.

Wow, that's…stark. Now I'm imagining it.

"S-so you're calling me an old hag?!" Fushimi was in shock.

"Uh, that's not what I… Actually, yeah, kinda." Torigoe showed no mercy.

Maybe the reason this is the only thing she can cook is because I like it. Maybe it's just coincidence. Although…if I told her I liked something else, would she learn how to make it?

I decided to test the theory later.

The picnic went on, and we were having a great time. I ate 90 percent of the pumpkin.

"Hina! Wanna play?" Mana took out the badminton rackets and shuttle she had brought.

"Sounds fun. Let's do it!"

They stood up and started rallying.

"Mana, why did you get into street fashion and stuff?"

"I just thought it was cute. Ha!"

"It wasn't Ryou, was it? Just kidding!"

"Isn't that exactly your...case?!"

"N-no, it's not. I just tried changing my looks over summer break, that's all."

"Ah-ha-ha. Now that's a bad excuse, Hina."

"Mmm…"

They were as friendly as ever. Each thwack of the shuttle was loud and clear; the two were talented at sports.

Meanwhile, Torigoe was doing whatever with her phone.

"Playing games?"

"No. Just messaging… Takamori, do you know this girl called Minami Shinohara?"

"Huh? Shinohara? Uh…yeah." I gave a vague answer.

We had gone to the same middle school. Or to be more specific…

She had confessed to me. And I'd said yes.

Why did she bring her up anyway?

"I was in grade school with her, and then we also ended up together in cram school for the entrance exams, and we've been talking since. You were in middle school with her, right?"

"Uh…yeah."

Minami Shinohara. Of course I knew her. She'd asked me out back then, and I'd said yes. I'm not sure we were what you'd call *a couple*, but that did technically happen.

"So—" Torigoe tried to ask something else, but Fushimi interrupted.

"Join us, you two!"

©Fly

"I brought rackets for all of us!"

They wanted us to play badminton.

"No, I'm fine."

Mana giggled. "Bubby, you don't have to feel bad about being a terrible player. We're not expecting you to wow us with your badminton prowess."

Urgh...

I couldn't back down after hearing that. "I'll have to get serious, then."

"You're so easy to manipulate, Bubby."

"Serious? Ryou? Is that even possible?" Fushimi quipped.

I stood up and grabbed one of the rackets. "Torigoe, you too. Let's play, all of us."

"Huh? I..." Fushimi and Mana also beckoned to her, so she stood up. "F-fine, just for a bit..."

Torigoe turned out to be more sociable than I thought. I was actually surprised she was here at all.

We stood in a circle and started rallying the shuttle. Torigoe and I sucked, to be frank, but Fushimi and Mana were skillful enough that it went on for a good while.

"It ended, and it's your fault for shooting all the way there, Bubby!"

"No, that was the wind's fault. Didn't you feel that sudden gust?"

"Don't worry about it, Takamori."

"Hold up, Torigoe. You're saying that as if it really was my fault."

"Don't worry about it, Ryou."

"You too, Fushimi?"

We played the blame game every time a rally stopped, and most of the time it ended with me getting the short end of the stick. Unforgivable. At least Torigoe was having fun.

"Speaking of which, you're not wearing your T-shit today, huh, Fushimi?"

"Hey, don't say that!"

"Did you mean to say 'T-shirt'?" Torigoe asked.

"Nope. It's fashion advice. Hina's taste in clothes is, well, shit!"

"Stop calling it that!"

"By the way, her outfit for today is entirely from the 'prestigious' fashion store Shiromura."

"Mana! Don't tell her that!"

Oh… So that's why she looks decent today.

She was wearing a nondescript long-sleeved T-shirt and a hoodie on top. For the bottom, she had a pair of jeans and sneakers for easy mobility. It was the most average outfit ever.

"You tried to come here wearing the dress Bubby bought you! Who even thinks about wearing their one and only nice outfit for a picnic? Consider the time, place, and occasion for, like, a second."

"Aw… I'm sorry…"

Torigoe then shot me a glance. "Takamori, I didn't know you could do that."

"Do what?"

"Gift something nice to a girl."

I didn't know what *"nice"* meant to her, exactly, but it was a bit embarrassing to think about now.

According to Hina, "You know how princesses always change their clothes when they sneak out to visit the town? You can't just show up here in princess fashion."

Spoken as a true member of the fashion police.

"So you shop at Shiromura, Fushimi?" asked Torigoe. She was wearing a thin cardigan, denim shorts, and black tights. This was my first time seeing her in something other than her uniform, and…she had pretty good fashion sense?

"No, that's just the story to make me more relatable."

That explanation only makes it worse.

"No, it's not just a story. It's true. Honestly, Hina, if anything should've been fictional, it was that travesty you showed up in earlier."

"I-it's not like expensive fashion is always better!" Fushimi snapped, although she didn't deny it.

"Hee-hee-hee. Hina, I don't think you have any room to talk about fashion. You're my puppet."

"Aw…"

"I shop at Shiromura, too. They have plenty of cute stuff." Torigoe lent a helping hand.

"Yeah… Yeah! Right?"

"Though I don't shop for outdoor clothing. Mostly loungewear."

"L-loungewear…"

Although the helping hand turned out to be holding a knife.

Fushimi hung her head, dejected.

Mana was disappointed, too. "I've failed as your producer…!"

"Shiromura has good stuff, too, so who cares?" I said without any thought, and that was when the fashion police came after me.

"Okay then, Bubby. Who do you think looks better today? Hina or Tori? Just tell me whose clothes you like more. Go on." Mana pushed them next to each other.

"Torigoe."

"Th…th-thanks," she muttered.

Any and all emotion left Fushimi's face. If there had been even a slight breeze, she might've crumbled to dust.

"Um, yeah, sure." Miss Mana took the L.

"Why have I never bought decent clothes…?"

Fushimi was getting seriously depressed, so Mana grabbed her shoulder tight.

"Hina, listen. People aren't born with fashion sense. It's something you have to train!"

"You're so wise…"

"You will still learn more and more."

"Yes, teacher…!"

They hugged each other tight, their teacher-student bond strengthened as never before.

"Fushimi, you can just ask the shop assistant for help, and they'll show you something nice most of the time."

"R-really…?"

Torigoe nodded. "Do you…want to go shopping together sometime?"

"Can I?"

"If you want to."

"Y-yes, please!"

Their bond also seemed to have strengthened.

All's well that ends well, I thought as I sat back down, then took a sip of tea.

Suddenly, someone's phone rang. It wasn't mine, or Fushimi's, or Mana's. So it had to be Torigoe's. I didn't mean to, but I ended up taking a look at the message that showed up on the display.

Shino
Can I come by?

Shino… I remembered seeing that handle somewhere, I thought as the display turned black again. "…Shino."

I checked my own phone and found the contact.

So it's really her…

Shino… Minami Shinohara. Torigoe had said she was friends with her—had they just been texting?

"Torigoe, your phone rang."

"Oh, okay."

Torigoe didn't care to look—maybe it wasn't anything important for her.

I lay down on the picnic blanket and looked at the sky.

Shinohara went to a private girls' school…I think. We'd ended up in different classes for third year, so I wasn't sure. We were together during second year, and at the end of fall that year was when she'd asked me out, after classes, near the school entrance.

Most likely, no one knew about us. We'd broken up before any rumors started spreading, after all. Three days. That was it; that was our whole relationship.

I counted her as an ex-girlfriend, since she did technically ask me out and I did technically say yes, but maybe to her, we weren't even that. Back then—and even now, to be honest—I didn't know what couples were supposed to do.

In fact, I think it was around that time that I started to get really confused with what it meant to be in love. Not that I ever got it, but that whole episode just muddled things further.

What did we do during those three days? Nothing. Honestly, I just spent them thinking, *Hmm, I wonder what we might do.* And in the end, she just said, *"Nope, can't do it."*

"'…Nope, can't do it…' Huh."

It's kinda funny thinking about it now. Back then, my mind went blank except for a bunch of question marks. She was the one asking me out, and then she'd said that.

Torigoe poured orange juice into her cup and sipped it while she watched the other two playing around.

"Did Shinohara say anything about me?"

"Like what?"

"Nothing… Never mind."

Yeah, this was kinda hard to ask about. If she didn't already know we (technically) dated, the news could come as a nasty shock.

"What's she like?" I asked instead.

Shinohara felt like an alien to me. The only thing I could remember about her at this point were her rimless glasses and her uniform.

"Mii is…"

"'Mii'?!"

Torigoe blushed. "Anything wrong about it? That's what I called her back in grade school."

"Sorry. I just wasn't prepared for that."

Torigoe cleared her throat before continuing. "We were best friends back in grade school."

"Oh, so you're childhood friends."

"No. Not like you and Fushimi anyway."

"Oh," I replied, still lying down.

"Takamori, are you curious about her?"

"Not really… I was just thinking about her, since you brought her up out of nowhere."

"You sure? You did ask, after all." She giggled. "She's kinda like Fushimi, although their personalities are pretty different."

"I know that, yeah. The type to be both smart and sporty."

"Exactly. Her face is like a fox's, and her personality is like a cat's."

"What does that even mean?"

The fox comparison was, well, workable. I could imagine that. Her sharper eyes and glasses gave off that cool beauty aura.

I still didn't understand why Shinohara liked me. I wasn't even sure she actually did in the first place.

We weren't in the same club, or working together for the school festival, or going through any sort of event that brought us closer. If anything at all, we were in the same group for the field trip. But our group didn't do anything special.

I was also really nervous when she'd asked me out, and I didn't understand what she said back then. It went something like, *"Let us follow the path of our fate…,"* and then, uhhh, what was it? Whatever, I just doubted someone was making her say it. She didn't even glance my way before that, and looking back, I didn't feel any passion or anything of the sort from that declaration. Her voice was really low, too.

Ah…

Then I realized. It all made sense. There was only one possible conclusion: It was a dare! Yes, it had to be part of some game with her friends.

"Oh, I see how it is now…"

"Huh? What? What's up?"

"Nothing." I turned my back to Torigoe.

Yeah. Now I get it.

It wasn't something I'd have been able to really notice back then when I was in the middle of the emotional storm, but now that I could think straight, I realized the truth. Of course she wouldn't like me. We'd barely spent any time together.

That also explained what she meant by, *"Nope, I can't do it."* It wasn't that she couldn't stand me but more exactly that she couldn't keep going with the dare.

"What kind of girl is Mii, from your point of view, Takamori?"

"A girl who follows the path of her fate."

"Excuse me?"

"I don't get it, either. Oh, and also that she's not the kind of girl to 'look pretty without her glasses.' She looks plenty pretty with glasses on."

"Oh yeah. I agree. Though those glasses are just for show, you know?"

Seriously? I didn't see that coming.

"She didn't use them back when we were in grade school, so once we reunited in cram school, I asked if her eyes got worse, and she said something like…, 'These aren't to correct my eyesight. You can see the world more clearly through a filter.'"

"Oh… A filter?"

"I dunno. I asked her for an explanation, but it didn't make much more sense."

"She can see more clearly with glasses for show…?"

Is that…possible? And are they really for show? Aren't they real?

The only thing I did know was that she'd played with my pure, young heart.

Yeah, I can't count her as an ex-girlfriend. Shoo, shoo.

Not that I had ever or would ever tell anyone. Good thing, too. Otherwise I'd be "that guy who took seriously some girl asking him out as a dare" forever.

"Dodged a bullet on that one…"

"What have you been muttering about for a while now?"

Torigoe tilted her head, puzzled.

SHII: What does "following the path of your fate" mean?

SHINO: huh?

SHINO: what's this about? lol

SHII: Takamori said it 😊

SHII: After I asked him what sort of girl you are to him

SHINO: takaryou?

SHINO: AAAAAAAAAAAAAAAAAAAAAAAAAAAAAAAAAAAAA

SHINO: I JUST REMEMBERED NOOOOOOOOOOOOOOOOOOOOO

SHII: What?

SHINO: don't ask 😆

SHII: Why?

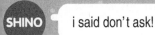

SHINO i said don't ask!

SHINO this is something i can never tell even you

The picnic ended without incident, the days went by, and now it was after school on Monday the week after.

"Fushimi, do you remember Minami Shinohara?" I asked her on our way home.

"Shinohara? Yeah, I do. She went to Seiryo, right?"

"I'm surprised you do, considering she was in another class for third year."

"Well, isn't my mind so bright?" she said with a smug face.

Seiryo University High School was the school's full name.

I doubted anyone besides us two in question would know anything happened between us. I hadn't talked to Fushimi like this back then, and I hadn't had any real male friends.

"We were in the same group for field trip in second year, so that's why."

Shinohara was in a similar position in class to Torigoe, what with people calling her boring or quiet or whatever.

"Why do you ask?"

The text from "Shino" saying "Can I come by?" on Torigoe's phone crossed my mind. Turned out, she didn't mean come by to see us but rather to visit Torigoe's house. We didn't see her then.

"Torigoe said they were classmates in grade school, and they're still friends."

"Oooh."

There was a reason why I'd abruptly brought her up.

"Wait. Stop changing the subject, Ryou."

"…"

We got back our English quiz results that day.

I had been taken by surprise back when we took it, although Fushimi assured me that Waka had warned us. I then told her she should've reminded me, to which the princess replied, *"Well, how would I know you didn't hear her tell us?"* She couldn't believe my ability to let things go in one ear and out the other.

"People who did poorly should be especially careful when midterms come around. I'll have you take extra lessons after school if you fail, all right?" Our English teacher, Miss Wakatabe, was ostensibly speaking to us, but her eyes were dead set on me.

From what I could tell by listening to the others talking about their results, apparently my score was the only one you could count up to on one hand.

"You'll have to spend all of Golden Week studying, Ryou."

"We still have time before midterms. I won't let studying ruin my holi—"

"You *never* study; that's why this happened, you know."

"Still…you think that's fair?"

Making me waste precious vacation time?

"I want to go out with you during Golden Week… You'll have to start studying right now if you want to have any chance of passing midterms…"

Fushimi dropped her shoulders, and I put a hand on one of them.

"Oh, don't worry."

"You *do* know who's worrying me right now, don't you?" She sighed.

Obviously I didn't want to lose my time to supplementary lessons. I did want to avoid failing, but, well…sometimes things are just hard. My test scores had been spiraling downward ever since high school started.

"I know!"

"What?" I turned to her, puzzled.

Fushimi's face was full of determination. "Let's study. And you don't get to say no."

"Huhhh?"

Seriously? Now? Even though there's no tests in sight? Not that I study even when there are...

"What do you mean, I don't get to say no? You're not robbing me of my freedom."

"Shut it, Mr. Three."

"Hey, that just means I've got ninety-seven whole points of potential growth ahead of me."

"You're not arguing your way outta this one, mister."

Ugh. So her super-serious side finally rears its stubborn head.

"B-besides...we haven't had much time to be alone together..."

"Huh?"

"N-n-nothing!" She shook her arms, her face red.

We're always alone together walking to and from school, though...

"Okay, so...we should start with your two worst subjects: English and math..."

She's already making a schedule!

"Can we create a five-year plan, Miss Fushimi...?"

"Ryou...when exactly are you thinking of graduating?"

"I just mean, please think long-term."

"No worries. I won't let you take extra lessons."

The confidence shining in her eyes gave me a very bad feeling.

Fushimi Cram School opened its doors immediately, in my house. She wouldn't back down no matter how vehemently I refused.

I dropped my bag, finally back in my own one-hundred-square-feet castle. On my desk was a note from Mana saying, I'll be late today, so make yourself something to eat. On top of it, the love glove.

"I don't need this, for crying out loud." I dunked it into the trash can.

"Can I come in now?"

"Y-yeah."

Thank God I made her wait outside.

I let her in, and she opened up her English textbook on my low table. She then took out from her bag a box the size of a pencil case.

What's that?

"Starting today, I'm your private tutor." She took a pair of glasses from the box and put them on.

"Did you buy them just for this...?"

"N-no, no! These are the ones I got when I was having trouble seeing the blackboard..."

I had never seen her wear glasses during class. Well, we weren't too far away from the blackboard this time, so maybe she just didn't need them.

"Let's do it, Ryou."

She was ready to go. There was no stopping her now. Fastest way through this was to take it seriously and study.

"Yeah, yeah," I answered while also taking out my textbook and notebook.

We started by reviewing that day's lesson, then progressively going back in time to find our starting point. We ended up having to use our first-year textbook.

"You just need to understand what the experts are trying to say here, and the test will be a piece of cake in comparison," the honor student said. "They base the tests on the most important points. You just need to get the core of it."

"...I'm starting to feel like I might make it."

"Right?" she said, smiling smugly for the umpteenth time while pushing up her glasses. "...Also, we promised we'd attend the same college."

"You mean when we were kids? Preschoolers possibly?"

Did we make that promise? Damn precocious kids.

"I mean, even if we didn't, I do think it would be fun if we could be together in college..." She was so earnest about this; I couldn't help watching her profile.

©Fly

"Yeah… I also think…that would be fun…I guess," I muttered.

Fushimi wasn't expecting that answer.

"" …""

We both blushed and stayed silent for a while.

"D-don't just say that out of nowhere," she whispered, then lightly whacked my arm. "I…I think that's enough for today."

She couldn't take it anymore and gathered her stuff, then left, her face still red up to her ears.

In the physics room during lunch break, I told Torigoe about Professor Hina being my private tutor, and she burst out laughing.

"You deserve that."

"No way! It was just a little quiz."

"And you got a *three*. You summoned Professor Hina yourself."

"What was your score, by the way?"

"And it's not like it was just a couple of questions. Really, a single-digit score goes beyond being funny; it's just sad."

"C'mon—just tell me."

"I'd rather look ahead. We've got midterms coming up, so I'm more worried about that than some little quiz."

She's not telling... Did she flunk it, too?

She doesn't strike me as the type, though. She usually answers correctly when the teachers ask her questions in class. Plus, she's always reading. But maybe I'm wrong.

Liking novels didn't mean you'd be good at English or math.

"Torigoe, want to join Professor Hina's classes?"

Having a comrade in the trenches with me would also make it easier to handle.

"No, it's fine. I don't want to get in the way."

"In the way? Of studying?"

"You are dumb as a brick, you know that?"

A brick? I mean, I'm not the sharpest tool in the shed, but there's no need to go that far.

"I'll ask her. I'll tell her you want to join."

"No, don't lie to her."

"Well, the truth is that I would like you to be there with me."

I grabbed my phone and asked with my eyes if I could text her about it, when Torigoe suddenly covered her face with both hands.

"Seriously… You're worse than a brick… Please don't say that to me."

I couldn't see her face, but her ears were red.

"Fushimi was in the top five all six times in midterms and end-of-term tests last year. I think it's probably easier to learn from her than the teachers."

"Good. Take your own advice."

"I have never cared about my own grades."

Torigoe laughed, but it was a frustrated kind of laugh. "Ha-ha-ha. And that's why she's making you study now, right?"

I never remembered promising to go to the same college as her, but it was a goal of mine now. I had no idea what I'd even want to study in college, but if I was gonna go anyway, what would be better than attending it together with her? Actually, I couldn't even imagine going to a school without her.

"Well, if you *insist*, I *suppose* I can study with you."

"There we go! Was that so hard?"

"I can study fine by myself. In fact, I think I'd be the one helping, especially after I was so politely asked…"

After she'd told me her feelings, Torigoe had taken a less polite, more sarcastic kind of tone with me. I took that to mean we'd gotten closer.

"Please help me study."

"Sure."

Despite the somewhat haughty attitude, she accepted right away. Now it was time to text Fushimi about it. I got a reply immediately: Of course! She's welcome anytime!

I told Torigoe about it.

"Tell her I won't stay too long and not to worry."

"Huh?"

I didn't get what she meant, but I passed on the message. I got a read notification but no reply.

"Now she's texting me. Really, you two are too sweet for your own good," Torigoe muttered to her phone.

After school, we finished writing the class journal and headed for the library.

"Ryou, do you get more motivation when you have a rival?"

"He just wanted to drag someone else into it," Torigoe retorted.

She was sharp. Damn.

"A-and it's not like it's any different for you whether you teach one or two people, right?" she added quickly.

We were the only ones left at the school library tables. No one else would stay here to study outside of test season.

Torigoe and I were sitting side by side, with Fushimi at the other end of the table. We once again started by reviewing today's class; then Fushimi explained whatever we didn't understand.

"Oh, not you too, Torigoe…"

"…!"

"Too"?

Fushimi had flipped through her textbook pages and pulled out the piece of paper hidden inside.

"That's your quiz results, right?"

"N-no."

"Twelve points…"

"Usually my intuition's better than that."

"I get it, Torigoe, I really do. Intuition is very important. But I thought you were smart. This score… I'm disappointed." I laughed.

Now Fushimi was mad. "You have no right to laugh at anyone, jerk."

"Yes, ma'am… I'm sorry."

She kicked me from below the desk, and I kicked her back.

"Hey!" she said. "Take this seriously. Focus on the exercise."

"You started it."

Torigoe sighed. "All right, I know you two like each other, but stop flirting under the table."

I was getting scolded again.

""We're not flirting!""

"Yeah, yeah. Lovebirds."

"I didn't know Torigoe was so cruel…" Fushimi was in shock.

Torigoe shook her head. "Sorry, I didn't mean it like that. I was just playing around."

"Well, stop playing around and start studying," I said.

"As if you've done any studying today—"

"Ryou," Fushimi interjected. "Please focus. I know you can do it."

What are you, my mom?

We ended our study session in the library once it was time for the school to close for the day. I kinda had a good time, honestly.

"Torigoe, if you don't mind, want to study with us again sometime?"

"Are you okay with me joining?"

"Yeah. It was fun." Fushimi gave her a warm smile.

"Okay… Sure," Torigoe answered shyly.

We found a girl standing near the school entrance once we got out. She wasn't wearing our school's uniform. Maybe she was waiting for her boyfriend to come back from club activities or something.

"Ah!" Torigoe exclaimed when she saw her. "Mii, what are you doing here?"

Mii? Now, where have I heard that name…?

"Long time no see, Shii."

Who's this?

"Ah, Shinohara? It's been so long," Fushimi said.

Shinohara? Wait… Minami Shinohara?

Her glasses had black frames now, her hair was longer than before, and she was wearing a different uniform, so I hadn't recognized her immediately. But upon closer inspection, it really was Minami Shinohara.

"Long time no see, Fushimi. And Takaryou."

Shinohara's catlike eyes shifted to Fushimi and then to me.

Why is she here? I wondered. "Y-yeah, long time."

"Ryou, what's the matter? You look nervous."

"No way, no." I reflexively massaged my face with both hands to relax it.

Torigoe and Shinohara started talking.

"Mii, why are you here?"

"I was just passing through, and I thought I'd stop by."

Shinohara had a cool aura that reminded me of Torigoe's; maybe it was the eyes and glasses.

Fushimi joined in the conversation, and while they were catching up, I was getting left behind.

…Which is totally fine. Let the girls chat among themselves.

"Okay then, I'll be going home—"

"We shouldn't just stand around here talking; how about we go to McB's?" Fushimi suggested, her eyes sparkling. Shinohara and Torigoe accepted after a moment's hesitation.

McB's was everyone's favorite burger place, by the way.

I glanced at Shinohara, and she stared right back at me. Truth be told, I was a bit afraid of her. She was like an alien to me; I had no idea what she was thinking.

"I—I have some stuff to do."

"No you don't," Fushimi countered. "You don't have anything to do after school."

"Hey, how do you know?"

©Fly

Exactly, completely right. What the hell?

"Well, if that's okay with you, Mii?"

"I don't mind."

"…"

No, please mind. It's kinda awkward here. Shouldn't you be the most sensitive to this stuff? Please.

Sadly, my thoughts didn't reach her. Fushimi and Shinohara started walking while the conversation continued.

"Hey, does Mii being here make it awkward for you? That's why you don't wanna go?"

Torigoe… I knew you would understand…

I looked up with hope at my goddess of salvation, after which she burst out laughing.

"Pffft. Yup. That's hilarious."

She's enjoying it!

"Of course not," I said, but she knew I was lying.

"I guess that's no surprise, after all you went through."

"Wait, did she tell you about us?"

"Yeah. She said you begged her to go out with you, said you would die if she didn't, but then three days later, you told her, 'Nope, can't do it.' Conceited prick."

Wait a second, that was backward. You *said all that, Shinohara! Don't pin that on me!*

"She told me to be careful around you."

"That damn Shinohara… This is slander!"

I was boiling mad now. I had to take my revenge.

We arrived at the McB's near the train station, ordered our food at the counter, then found an open table on the second floor. I just got an order of fries, while the girls had ice cream.

"Ryou, you're so considerate. We can alternate between sweet and salty so they both taste even better." Fushimi giggled after taking a lick of her ice cream, then grabbed one of my fries.

After getting up to speed with everyone, Shinohara asked, "Fushimi, Takaryou, you're not dating, right?"

She glanced at me, then her, then back at me.

"Nope," I answered without hesitation.

Fushimi, with the stoic mask of a monk, poked my side.

Stop it.

"I see," Shinohara said and gave her ice cream another lick.

"By the way, Mii, did you get new glasses? They were rimless back in middle school."

"Koff, koff," she choked.

Fushimi took out her handkerchief and tried handing it to her. "Are you all right?"

"Yes, thank you." Shinohara waved off the handkerchief and cleared her throat. "Y-yeah, I changed them."

"And do you see the world more clearly now?" Torigoe had a slight smile on her face.

"…It's none of your business." Shinohara looked away.

"What does it look like to you now?" Torigoe didn't back down, while Shinohara was starting to sweat.

Wait…I don't think they're talking about it in a physical sense.

"What? What are you two saying?" Fushimi asked, puzzled.

Torigoe pressed her lips together, as if trying to stifle laughter.

Oh, she's evil.

So I guessed Shinohara was, y'know, suffering from a certain affliction you see a lot of in anime and manga. The one that usually affects middle school boys.

"…Well, there is that stereotype that people with glasses are timid and boring. Were you trying to act like wearing them was inevitable?"

My theory seemed to hit home—Shinohara turned into a waterfall of sweat.

Yup, this is what we call survivor of the dramatic edgy teen phase.

It made sense now. No wonder that line she said about *"following the path of our fate"* sounded right out of some anime.

"Shinohara, you're sweating a lot—are you okay? Your ice cream is melting. You should follow the path of your fate."

Her shoulders jumped up, and then Torigoe noticed I had noticed.

"Mii, why are you sweating? Just follow the path of your fate."

Shinohara twitched again, her face burning red. Meanwhile, Fushimi had a ton of question marks on top of her head, looking at us like a fidgety prairie dog.

Shinohara pushed up her glasses and handed me her ice cream.

"Here, you have this, Takaryou. I—I'm going home…" She grabbed her bag and stood up.

"See you!" Fushimi waved at her, completely oblivious.

Although it was Torigoe who'd started it, maybe I went too far. But that's what she deserved for slandering me. She got off easy, really.

I opened my mouth to lick my free ice cream, but Fushimi snatched it out of my hand. "I'll take that."

"Hey, you've got your own already."

"This… Well… You can have mine."

"Why does it matter?"

Then, Torigoe offered me her cone, too. "Want mine, then?"

"As I said… Why does it matter?"

Why do they all want Shinohara's ice cream so bad?

Confused, I looked at the window. Right then, I saw Shinohara walking away outside. She turned around and noticed I was looking at her. She mouthed, *Asshole*, then turned around, her long hair waving.

Even if you ignored the fact that this was our first conversation in years, she was truly incomprehensible.

"Hey, they're staring at you."

"Let them. I don't care."

Fushimi saw Shinohara chatting with me and tapped the desk with her finger.

"No talking."

""Yes, ma'am.""

Fushimi, Torigoe, and I had been studying in the city library after school when Shinohara happened to come by. You didn't find many kids here in a Seiryo uniform, so she was getting a lot of double takes.

"Good thing we all use the same textbook," Torigoe said.

Yeah, Shinohara wouldn't have been able to join us otherwise.

"Why did you even come? Yesterday too."

"Does it bother you? Why do you care?"

We talked sneakily while solving our English exercises, trying not to anger the strict Professor.

She had said she was *"just passing through"* the day before, and now she showed up here *"by chance,"* but that was a lot of coincidences, wasn't it?

I suspected Torigoe, the "Shii" to her "Mii." But she didn't seem like a bad person, so I decided to let it go for the time being.

"Who actually goes to study at the library?"

"Well, where are you now, Takaryou? Midterms are soon anyway, so yeah. Besides, why is it so bad to want to be with friends?"

"I mean, it's not, but…," I muttered.

"Mr. 'Takaryou,' please focus on your studying," the ruthless Professor scolded me again.

I obeyed and focused on solving the exercise.

Our study session lasted until just before closing time. We were there for about two hours, breaks included. It was pretty refreshing after focusing for so long.

Fushimi and Torigoe chatted while Shinohara and I followed behind them.

"I never knew that side of Fushimi even existed."

"She's pretty different from how she acts in the classroom."

"It felt like she was wearing a mask back in middle school."

I knew what she meant. She had this smile on all the time, with everybody. I'm sure some of them noticed it wasn't real.

"Do you have feelings for Fushimi?"

"Bw-whut?!" I choked.

"You, like, *like* her? Love her, even?"

"I don't know. And it's all your fault, y'know?"

"Mine? Don't pin that on me."

"You treated me like a toy. Maybe I should've done something about it, but I just didn't know what was up back then."

"Well…" Shinohara pondered.

"They made you do it, right?"

"Huh?" Her eyes widened, and she blinked several times.

"You lost a game with some friends, and they dared you to ask me out, right?"

"Um… Y-yeah!"

I knew it.

The whole incident was three years ago now, so I wasn't planning on telling her off for it. I was just relieved the mystery had been solved.

"Yeah, that's what I expected."

"Uh-huh…"

"Of course you would break up after three days with someone you were forced to ask out."

"…Are you mad about it?"

"I wasn't even mad back then, so no. I'm just glad to finally know why that happened."

"But…that's not what…"

"What?"

"N-no, nothing!" She shook her head vehemently. "I didn't know you thought that all this time…"

"They didn't bully you or anything, did they?"

"Huh?"

"Did they?"

"N-no. That much is true."

"Good."

I smiled, glad to have my worries dispelled for good.

"Awww… Now I feel bad…"

"Huh?" I turned with a puzzled expression.

"Forget that. I just thought you hated me all this time. It is true that I was unfair to you. That's why I was feeling so on edge yesterday…"

Ah, so that's why she was so aggressive.

"Those three days were like a storm."

Three years had already gone by since then. I'd felt awkward all during the school day, then worried about going home together, in case the other guys made fun of me. I'd never felt that way before or since.

"…"

Shinohara walked beside me, silent and hunched. I could tell her face was red, even in the poor light.

"Why did you suddenly get so close to Fushimi?"

"It wasn't suddenly… We've been friends since we were kids."

"Coulda fooled me back in middle school."

And during the first year of high school, to be honest.

"Sorry. I don't mean to put you down. Although…she may not be showing you who she really is, either." She lowered her volume for that last part.

I replied similarly. "What do you mean?"

"I just thought that maybe that's another mask she's wearing."

"…"

"You go to and from school together, right? What do you think she's doing when she's not with you?"

"Well…"

Huh? Studying, I guess? But wait, the other day she said simply paying attention in class was enough for her to know what's important and what's not, so I doubt she spends her entire time studying.

"Huh…? I wonder."

"Right?"

I felt the distance between us widening yet again. Even though she was right there in front of me.

"How about you try asking her next time?"

"Um, sure… I'll try."

I always figured she'd say something like, *"I was watching TV," "I was on my phone," "I was doing homework,"* so I never bothered asking. But now, thanks to Shinohara, I wasn't so sure.

"Though I doubt she's doing anything…intense. Not her."

"What do you mean by that?"

"…Don't make a lady say it out loud, jerk."

Something "intense" that a "lady" shouldn't be saying…

"No, there's no way."

She doesn't mean…

We parted ways with Torigoe and Shinohara near the station, while we got on the train. We sat together in some open seats.

"Ryou, you'll be totally fine at midterms if you keep your focus up just like today!" Fushimi nodded in satisfaction with total confidence. "I know you can do it when you put your mind to it."

"Stop it, Mom."

Fushimi giggled, and I figured it was a good chance to ask her.

"Hey, Fushimi. What do you usually do on weekends? Like, when you're not with me or Mana. I just wondered."

"Huh? On weekends? Well... On weekends, I..."

Wh-what is it? You're not watching TV or browsing your phone or doing homework...?

"Wait! Please give me some time before I can tell you that. Sorry."

"Wh-why?"

"I, um... I need to prepare myself for it."

Oh no. What bomb are you going to drop on me? Why do you need preparation to tell me something like this?

Once again, I was spending lunch break in the physics room. I asked Torigoe what had been on my mind since the day before.

"Do you know what Fushimi does when she's alone?"

"No. Who cares, though? Everyone has time alone, right?"

Well…yeah.

I shoved an entire piece of Mana's handmade rolled egg in my mouth to give me some time to think. Torigoe didn't know and didn't care.

What could she possibly mean by having to *"prepare herself"* to tell me? Sure, that technically meant she was fine telling me, but why was it such a struggle?

"Maybe she's doing something…intense."

"No. There's no way." I immediately turned to look at Torigoe.

"It's a joke. Don't take it so seriously."

Her calm comeback made it awkward, so I kept my mouth shut after that.

"Girls have lots of things to take care of," she went on, "unlike you sloppy boys."

"What do you mean?"

"Like, self-improvement or something?"

I cracked a smile. I wasn't expecting such a pretentious word to come out of her mouth.

"I think Fushimi's the type of person to put in the effort while no one's looking, so you never know."

"You think so?"

"Yeah. She's one of those types who's like, 'Oh no, I haven't studied at all, I'm gonna fail,' right before exams, even though she studied her butt off at home, y'know?"

"Oh…"

Yeah, I've heard her say that in the classroom.

"Self-improvement, huh… Well, truth be told, I did ask her, but then she told me she needed some time to prepare herself to tell me."

"What?" Torigoe seemed puzzled.

I'd asked Mana the same thing the day before, and she lectured me. *"Bubby, what are you doing? Are you the possessive type? Don't do that. Don't assume you should be the only one to know every facet of her life."*

Shinohara said it's likely she was wearing a mask even when talking to me, and there was no way of saying. The chances of her putting on the childhood-friend mask weren't exactly zero.

"Wanna tail her, then?"

I accepted the suggestion and met with Torigoe and Shinohara at the station on Sunday.

"This is kinda exiting," Shinohara said, bringing sweet red-bean buns for all of us. She was totally into this detective thing.

"What was she doing yesterday?" Torigoe asked.

"We played games with Mana at my house, read manga. Nothing special."

"Like true childhood friends."

"Indeed."

Fushimi had told me she had plans for Sunday, so we got together on Saturday instead. I asked Torigoe and Shinohara about it and found out her plans weren't with any of them, so I guessed something was up. And so, here we were.

We headed to Fushimi's house just as we saw her go out. We hid wherever we could and followed her.

"Where is she going?"

No one answered my question. We stealthily tailed her and got on the bus. She got off at Hamadani, the shopping district we'd gone to before.

"W-wait for me... I don't use a card... I gotta pay for the ticket...," Shinohara said in a panic, searching for her ticket and wallet in front of the gate.

"We're leaving. We're gonna miss her."

"Hey...wait."

I left her behind. *Sayonara.*

Torigoe wasn't far behind; she felt bad about leaving her, but her curiosity won out.

"Your sis wasn't wrong about her fashion sense... Is she really okay walking around Hamadani dressed like that? Where's her pride as a high school girl?" Torigoe was having secondhand embarrassment. "Oh. Or maybe that's her way of being funny? Like she does it on purpose?"

"She was literally crying when she told us that it was not a joke, so please don't ever say that to her."

We kept following her through the main street until she entered an alleyway and then a building containing a variety of businesses.

"What if she *is* doing something...intense?"

"Please stop it. I just thought the same thing."

The building was quite big and held various tenants: There was an ikebana place and a tea ceremony place on the third and fourth floors, all sorts of cultural centers. The list of tenants helped me relax a little. Torigoe too, I think.

The old elevator Fushimi got into stopped at the fourth floor, where they had calligraphy classes, math for children, and various other conference rooms.

We told our bun-delivery girl where we were and went up to the fourth floor. The entire floor was silent save for a couple of voices—the calligraphy and math teachers. Their voices got louder as we approached the classrooms. Then someone came out of a different room: a boy who appeared to be in his later years of grade school. He was going to the restroom. What class was he here for?

"Takamori, look. He was in here." Torigoe pointed at the classroom's nameplate: HAMADANI THESPIAN ACADEMY.

"Huh. Thespian Academy? Thespian…"

"Yeah. You think Fushimi's in here?"

"Hey…what's 'thespian' mean?" I asked, my poor brain unable to understand the English name of the classroom.

Torigoe was equally as stumped.

"Look it up on your phone. You can find anything on the Internet."

Just say you don't know, either.

The boy came back from the restroom and gave us suspicious looks as he passed by. He opened the door, and for a second there, I saw her. No one but her would wear such a crappy T-shirt around this business district.

"So Fushimi's attending a *thespian* school," Torigoe commented, unfazed. As if she knew what she was talking about.

"Yeah, that isn't anything bad, right? Why hide it?"

"I know."

The conversation was a bunch of nonsense; we had no idea what we were talking about.

"I finally caught up to you," the bun-delivery girl said, out of breath. "Is Fushimi here?"

""Yeah.""

"Ah," she replied. "Yeah, I can see why she would have a hard time telling you. Wouldn't want you making fun of her or giving her any weird looks."

""Yeah, of course.""

Shinohara stood on her toes to try and peek inside. "So…I guess this is affiliated with some agency or something?"

""Agency…""

"The other girls would probably get jealous if they found out, too. I can totally see why she wouldn't say."

""So true.""

"I wonder if she wants to be a regular actress or a voice actor."

""Huh?""

"Yeah…you know… Drama school…?"

Our mouths shut after finally hearing the definition. Meanwhile, the vocal exercises filtered out of the classroom.

We left the building and went to a nearby café.

"I don't think it's that unexpected." Torigoe blew on her latte before taking a sip.

"You think so?" I asked.

"Yeah, I can see why Shii would say that." Shinohara also agreed. "There's no girls like that even in Seiryo."

"Really?"

I'd been saying nothing but *"You think so?"* and *"Really?"* for a while now.

Neither Torigoe nor Shinohara found it the least bit strange that Fushimi was trying to become a celebrity. As for me, I was conflicted. Fushimi had just told me we promised we'd go to college together.

"But Fushimi was saying she'd go to college."

"Some actors do go to college."

"Oh."

Well, of course she was thinking about her future. We were already in our second year of high school. You had to know your dreams and give them your all, or at least go to college if you still weren't sure what to do.

"…"

Torigoe glanced at me. "You've been awfully silent for a while now."

"You think so?"

"Lemme guess," said Shinohara. "You're sad about it? 'Nooo, then she won't be *my* Hina!'"

I didn't have enough energy to get back at her for laughing at me.

"No, I don't."

"Maybe you don't see it like that, since you're with her every day, but I'd say Fushimi is the prettiest girl in the entire prefecture, you know?"

"Oh, no need to tell me."

I know that.

"So a girl of that caliber is gonna be drawn to the spotlight, right?"

"I…guess."

I didn't sound convinced. But why?

It was like I'd been avoiding this for so long, but now it was right in front of me. I wanted to become…something. But I couldn't pin it down to anything more specific. I didn't know how big this thing was or what shape or color. I had no idea. Meanwhile, Fushimi already had this *something* inside her, and I still couldn't see it after so long at her side. Maybe that was why. Fushimi had *something* that wasn't her smarts, her athletic ability, or her looks, and that *something* was available to anyone. And it came as a surprise to me.

"…Fushimi isn't mine. She can do whatever she wants."

Both of them stared at me.

"Did you hear that, Shii? 'She isn't mine.'"

"S-stop that."

Shinohara gave Torigoe a light kick and got a poke in return.

I took a sip of my cream-and-sugar coffee. The sweet flavor washed over my tongue as I wondered if Fushimi could already drink black coffee. I knew how she was back then, but I knew barely anything about her now.

"Let's keep this a secret, okay? No one should mention it until she tells us."

"I know," I replied.

Fushimi wanted to be ready before telling me, which meant she could do it anytime.

"Ah, I have some plans for today, so I'm heading out," Shinohara said. She stood up and delivered our buns.

Right, we didn't eat these.

As she left, we said good-bye through the window.

"I wonder what Fushimi wants to be. An actress?"

"I guess."

"Hee-hee. Are you jealous?"

"I'm not. Who'd I be jealous of?"

"I wonder." She smiled.

I felt uncomfortable. Transparent.

"Or is this envy more like a grudge?"

"Okay, let's stop this conversation now."

"All right," she said, her smile even bigger than before, and stirred her almost-empty cup. "Stupid Mii…"

I asked what she meant with a glance, but she shook her head. So instead I asked, "What are you doing after this? It's only eleven."

"You're not going home?"

"Oh… Well, I can go, if that's what you want."

"Huh…? Would you come with me if I asked you?"

"Yeah, if there's anywhere you wanna go. We're already out here anyway."

"Then give me a second." She hurriedly did a search on her phone. "What about…here? If you'd be so kind?"

"Why so polite all of a sudden?"

I looked at the phone screen. It showed a map to a big bookshop nearby.

"Oh, sure. Yeah."

"They have all sorts of books in here, and they have the best selection of manga around these parts…"

That caught my attention, and our destination was set.

"It's really big, so be careful."

"Careful about what?"

"Getting lost."

"How old do you think I am?"

"No, I mean me…"

"*You're* worried about getting lost?" I burst out in laughter.

"I'm terrible with directions… I often can't tell where I am or where I'm heading, even in places I know."

Now, that was surprising. She didn't seem like the type.

"So please, take me there…"

"Oh, so that's why you broke out the map."

Now I see.

I checked her phone again, making sure where to go. Thankfully, it seemed to be only about a five-minute walk; there was no need to worry about getting lost.

"One of my favorite authors released a new book, and I want to check it out."

It started raining as soon as we got out of the café. The sky was dark, warning us of a heavier storm to come. We found a convenience store nearby and split the cost of one umbrella.

"Are you sure I can get under it with you?"

"You paid for it, too; of course you can use it."

"…You're right. Thanks…," she murmured, stepping under the umbrella at an appropriate distance.

The rain got heavier, but we reached the bookshop without trouble. I shook the umbrella dry before the entrance, when Torigoe turned to look at me in slight dissatisfaction.

"…That was closer than I thought."

"Yeah. Which is a good thing, since we didn't have to spend much time in the rain."

Fly

"…I wouldn't have minded if it were farther."

"Well, I don't want to get wet."

Torigoe was already inside the store by the time I said that.

It was a big place, taking up an entire five-story building. I went looking for series I was interested in at the manga corner, while checking if there were any new volumes of ones I was already following. This would take about ten minutes in a regular bookstore, but just as Torigoe had said, their selection was so huge, I ended up spending almost an hour.

Torigoe wandered off, probably to check out the novels on the second floor. I felt stupid for considering for even one second the possibility of this being a date. Like, I felt it just made more sense for us to go our own ways, then reunite later. No need to worry about boring the other when you just want to wander around aimlessly, either.

"…"

Then I found her in a corner of the giant floor. *Weren't you in the novels section?* She immediately noticed me, too.

"Oh, sorry. I imagined you might want to look at some dirty manga, so I thought it would be best to go our separate ways."

"Oh, come on. Don't assume I'd automatically look for porn."

I would never do something so risky when accompanied by a girl from my class. And on that note, the manga in Torigoe's hand seemed quite… intense.

"I was thinking about recommending this to Fushimi. Yeah, it's BL."

"And you don't care at all about *me* finding *you* looking at dirty manga?"

The cover showed two good-looking guys, chests bare, holding each other.

"I don't want to recommend it if she wouldn't like it, but there was this one novel that you could read as gay romance. She said she liked it."

So you're sensing some latent potential within Fushimi.

"I was also talking to Mii about how that novel totally counts as BL."

You too, Shinohara?

"In conclusion: BL is literature."

That's...deep? I think? I dunno.

"Wanna read it, too, Takamori?"

"No, thanks. What if I end up learning something about myself?"

"I...wouldn't like that, no."

"Well, there you go." I sighed.

The stares I was getting from the women in this area were starting to hurt. I returned to the section I was in before, and I suddenly felt my heart go back to normal. That was like accidentally wandering into the lingerie section.

"I guess that's how they get you into that stuff."

It was perfectly fine as a way to grow closer to your friends, but I had a hard time picturing Fushimi getting really into it.

I grabbed one manga I had been interested in and a new volume of another series and paid for them. Torigoe had also finished by then—I saw her in line for the register.

After we left the store, we wandered around for about an hour.

"I'm hungry."

It was already past noon. We checked our remaining money and found we still had some left, so we decided to eat and take a break at a family restaurant.

"What was it like when you dated Mii?" Torigoe asked while we were waiting for our Hamburg steaks to arrive.

"We didn't date. She just asked me out because they dared her."

"What?" Torigoe suddenly raised her face from her phone. "But you said you'd die if she didn't date you."

"You think I would be anywhere near that mushy?"

"Now that you mention it..." She looked puzzled.

"Shinohara told you the story backward. Whatever she said I did, she was the one who did it."

"...No wonder it sounded so strange."

The waitress's voice announced the arrival of our food, and I dug in while telling Torigoe everything I knew.

"…And so she broke up with me three days later."

"Oh… So you didn't do anything together?"

"We didn't even hold hands."

"I see," she said as she sliced her steak, then took the piece of meat to her mouth with a fork.

Knives were too much of a hassle for me, so I just used chopsticks.

"I see; I see," she said again.

Why three times?

"It sounds very like her. She's pretty stubborn—she doesn't like giving people the idea that she's not in control at all times. I guess that's why she'd be too embarrassed to say… It's like her dark past that she doesn't want known."

"Who're you claiming has a dark past?"

Torigoe giggled. She grabbed a sautéed piece of carrot with her fork and ate it.

"Have you kissed?"

"Of course not."

"You've never kissed anyone? Not even Fushimi?"

That time we butted heads on the train crossed my mind, but that didn't count. It was an accident.

"No."

"I see," Torigoe said yet again. The lack of emotion on her face made me feel like a bug under a microscope.

"What about you?" I asked. "Have you had your first kiss?"

"What do you think?"

"I dunno—maybe you'll surprise me."

"I wonder."

"Oh, c'mon. I told you."

"I'll leave that up to your imagination."

"What? Boooring."

Torigoe laughed, then immediately put on a serious face. "Do you think it'd be weird if I hadn't?"

"There are lots of early-bloomer girls, so I'd say there's more of them with experience than boys, but I wouldn't say it's weird…"

You shouldn't be talking about this with me. Though I don't really mind.

"There'd be this girl in the restroom talking about how she'd kiss her boyfriend, and people would ask about what happened next, and she'd start bragging about it; then everyone would be like, 'Oh, I totally get that.' But I don't get it. I'll sometimes wonder and imagine what it would be like to do that with someone I like, but I just can't bring myself to want to actually say it out loud and share it with my friends."

What it would be like to do that with someone you like…?

"…"

"Why are you red all of a sudden?"

"Nothing."

She probably didn't mean it that way, but my mind ended up wandering to her lips. She shrugged and went on. "Those girls talk like they're in some manga. And the ones listening ask for more and more detail. And I wonder if I would've gotten to live that manga fantasy if I'd gone for it a month ago."

"Don't tell me those things."

"Sorry. I don't say it to be mean. You're just easy to talk to."

"I'm glad you think so."

I stood up to go fill my drink at the soda fountain, and there I ran into Fushimi's dad.

"Oh, Ryou," he said.

"Oh, good evening."

Tsunehisa Fushimi wore round glasses, and his expression was as gentle as ever. His face was quite fine-looking—Fushimi had clearly inherited her parents' best traits.

He was there with the boy we'd found while following Fushimi, along with Fushimi's mom. Guess they'd come there to eat after acting class ended. Their table was near ours.

"Hina came here with us, but then she suddenly said she wanted to go back home."

"Is that so?"

That was when I noticed you could clearly see our table from theirs.

Mr. Tsunehisa told me about how he'd go see her lessons from time to time.

"Oh, you didn't know? That's a surprise. I would've assumed she'd tell you. Truth be told, I'm not exactly in favor of all this, but if it's what she wants, I'll support her how I can." He smiled.

I wondered if that conflict I felt was because she hadn't told me or something else entirely.

I returned to my seat, and Torigoe glanced at where I had been standing just before while taking a sip of orange juice.

"Who's that guy?"

"Fushimi's dad."

"Oh."

"Torigoe, do you have any plans for after high school?"

"Plans?"

"Yeah."

"Well... You know, now I kinda get how Fushimi feels and why she didn't say," Torigoe said, stirring her orange juice with the straw for no apparent reason.

"What do you mean?"

"That it's not the kind of thing you go around saying. Not like we're the main characters of some manga for boys. Who goes around yelling their ambitions at everyone?"

"That's...true."

"So her plans feel even more grounded because she doesn't share them. Words like *dreams* and *ambitions* feel really flimsy; her ideas about the future are more solid than that."

That was a perfectly fair, well-thought-out argument from Torigoe. At least it sounded reasonable to me, enough to understand why Fushimi wouldn't tell me.

"It's the kind of thing you keep to yourself, don't you think?" Torigoe said with a rare smirk, confident about how insightful her comments sounded.

"Mr. Tsunehisa—er, Fushimi's dad said she'd do live performances."

"She seems dedicated, a hard worker. I'm sure she'd succeed as an actress for TV, VA, or stage plays. She could do anything."

The words hit harder than I expected. Why?

"...Guess so," was the only thing I could say.

Torigoe then changed the subject, and we didn't talk about it anymore. She sure was chatty that day, despite not usually speaking much in the physics room. Even got me talking more than usual.

We left the restaurant in the evening, then went our separate ways at Hamadani Station. We had to take trains in opposite directions. She boarded hers first, and our eyes met through the window. She bashfully waved good-bye, and I returned the gesture.

Then my phone beeped with a text from Torigoe.

Thank you for going out with me today. I had fun.

You're welcome, I replied. My text immediately got marked as read.

Then I got another one—from Fushimi.

You went out with Torigoe today? You should've invited me!

I could easily picture her pouting.

I heard you were at the restaurant. You should've joined us.

Left on read.

How was I supposed to invite you when you were busy with classes? I typed but immediately deleted it.

I could tell we were having curry for dinner as soon as I got near my house. I parked my bike at the spot beside the garage and entered my home, heading first for the kitchen, where I found my mom stirring a pot of curry.

"No hello?" she asked.

"You first."

"Hello, then."

"Hi."

She had the night shift that day, according to the shift schedule on the fridge.

"Hey, Mom, why did you become a nurse?"

"Why do you ask?"

"Just because."

She eyed me like a mischievous cat. "Oh my, oh my. Oh, to be young again."

"Oh, come on. It's not what you think."

"Now that's adolescence talking. Oh nooo, the rebellious teeeeens."

You don't sound scared.

"I wonder why I did," she went on.

"You forgot?"

"Please, I'm not that old." She glared at me. "Just, no specific reason, I guess."

"Is that so…?"

"By the way, we're having my curry tonight. Not Mana's curry."

"Yeah, yeah," I replied again.

Mana was staying at a friend's house.

"She ran out crying, 'Bubby doesn't pay me any attention, so I'm never coming baaack!'"

"Yeah, I can see that."

"She'll make a great wife one day. Cute face, nice boobs…"

Was there any need for that last comment?

I finished my mom's curry and left my seat to go laze around in my room. There, I got a call from Fushimi.

"What's up?"

"Dad let me know he told you everything."

"Oh…you mean your classes?"

"Yeah. I didn't plan to hide it. I was thinking about telling you one day."

I couldn't confess to her the truth that I'd found out by myself and not through her dad.

Fushimi then told me about why she had chosen that path. It all started with a play she saw in middle school. She was impressed by the passionate and emotional acting and started dreaming about doing that herself.

"I didn't know that."

"Yeah. That's a side of me you didn't know."

What was I supposed to say to that?

"True, it's not like we both know everything about each other."

"I'm sure there are sides of you I don't know."

"Sure there are," I said.

We were apart for four whole years, so of course we'd still have more to learn.

"What do you think about me taking those classes? Honestly?"

I answered with Torigoe's previous comment.

"I think you can make it. TV or stage play or whatever else you want."

Fushimi laughed bashfully. *"Thank you,"* she said. *"I haven't told anyone, but I want to be an actress."* The declaration really was like the protagonist of a boys' manga.

◆**Hina Fushimi**◆

I locked my phone after my call with Ryou.

"…"

I couldn't ask him about it.

I saw them together at the restaurant the moment we entered. It was only a little bit before I told Dad I was going home. Torigoe was talking so much, and so was Ryou. They seemed to be having fun.

I didn't have the courage to walk up to their table. I can read the room. But I didn't even want to be near them. Why were they there, without any other friends? Why hadn't Ryou told me he'd be going out that day? Just hearing their voices sent all kinds of questions spinning through my head.

I bought that manga I told you about. I'll give it to you later.

Torigoe texted me.

She had asked Ryou out and gotten a no, but that didn't mean her feelings had gone away. Still, I'd thought his and my relationship was safe.

"Why can't things just go right all the time?"

Life's so hard.

I didn't even want to see Torigoe now. I'd said I would win him eventually, but now I was starting to lose confidence. Ryou told me that he felt best with me by his side, but…maybe the seat closest to him wasn't mine yet.

He was also very quick to say that we weren't dating when Shinohara had asked.

Couldn't you have hesitated for, like, a second?

I lay down on my bed and buried my face in my pillow.

"Be less sure, you jerk..."

I opened the texting app and typed a reply to Torigoe.

Thank you! I'm looking forward to it! That didn't feel right. It was too typical, too much. I deleted it.

Thanks. That's it? Too indifferent. Delete.

There were no bookstores near Torigoe's house; I knew that because she had once complained about it to me. Which meant that she had bought that manga today.

Did you have fun on your date with Ryou? Now this was it—how I really felt. But...I deleted it. I couldn't just say that.

She was never that excited talking to me. We had shared interests, so it wasn't like we were bored, but...

"Well, of course."

I knew how that felt. I got much more excited chatting with the one I loved, too.

◆Shizuka Torigoe◆

I bought that manga I told you about. I'll give it to you later.

She'd read my text but hadn't replied to me yet. Maybe she didn't know which manga I was referring to. I looked up the manga's website, sent her the link, and immediately regretted it; maybe I was being too aggressive. The first few pages were free, so I sent her that link.

Look.

I started typing out how and when I had brought it up before to help her remember, but then I stopped. I was getting too anxious. Maybe it was the guilt for going out with the guy my friend was in love with, even though it had been perfectly natural to do so from my point of view.

But…I still liked him, too. That unbelievably dense guy who sometimes blurted out things that made my heart jump out of my chest.

I didn't know when her classes would end, and I'd assumed we wouldn't bump into her, so I pushed for the date at the bookstore. We were supposed to keep the whole "tailing Fushimi" thing a secret, so Takamori definitely wouldn't talk about it. It would've been our own little secret. But things don't always go as expected. The guilt started building up inside me once I knew Fushimi had been at the restaurant. She wouldn't have gone home if seeing us hadn't bothered her.

"I have such bad luck…"

It was as if our friendship wasn't meant to be. We had some chemistry in certain aspects, but then there was this. I didn't know how to make the friction stop. Besides, it didn't feel right to apologize.

What did you two do after I left? Mii asked.

I could see her grinning right about then. Her choice to leave the two of us alone was a good move, though, so I thanked her in my mind.

I explained what had happened after, including the incident with Fushimi, then sent a sticker of a bear with a serious face, sweating. Then two more of the same.

So now I'm the bad guy.

Not if they're not dating.

Technically, I guess.

What do you suggest I do, my trusted strategist?

No idea.

So much for my trusted strategist.

Takaryou's the bad guy actually. Lol

True lol

No but really. What were you supposed to do? You still like him, right?

Seeing that written out made it even more embarrassing.

I don't think Takaryou can handle the princess anyway.

There it was. That was the unease I'd felt from Takamori's reaction. *"He can't handle her"* was the perfect way to put it.

I wonder.

This was a glimmer of hope for me, but I sent back a negative reply anyway. I really had no confidence, huh.

On one side we have a big sunflower that gets everyone's attention. On the other, a dandelion on the side of the road.

She didn't have to tell me who was who in this metaphor.

That's the difference between you two.

I feel the need to argue back, but I can't even deny it. RIP

It's true.

This would be an exciting development for a boys' manga, though.

…If only life were a manga.

Yeah. If this were a manga, I'd be able to make my grand comeback.

You often hear about how childhood friends have been so close since they were little that they're like family, but in truth, the tiniest event could trigger them to move on to the next step, and they had plenty of chances for it to happen. It was like cheating. But I had no choice except to fight back until the day one of them gave up or I stopped liking him.

Even though we were friends, we had ended up falling for the same guy. There was no way around it. What happened before was just round one. I'd lost the battle but not the war.

"I want to have a barbecue," Fushimi said with a completely serious expression.

"Uhhh…" I wasn't sure about that.

Torigoe, on the other hand, seemed weirdly on board. "Yeah, sounds good."

You could tell from her eyes that she was much more excited about it than she sounded.

Fushimi had brought this up as we were talking about what to do for Golden Week, which was coming up in just a few days—although technically we should've been studying.

"Right? You just can't leave out an opportunity for barbecue with your friends," Fushimi assured.

"Right?" Torigoe repeated.

"Though just the three of us would feel a little lonely."

"Let's call Shinohara, too."

"Then we get Takamori's sis, so we're up to five."

"There we have it!"

They nodded at each other.

I guessed they both had a desire to make this barbecue thing happen. Fushimi rarely hung out with friends like this, and that probably went for Torigoe, too. And me, technically, but the whole event sounded like more trouble than fun in my opinion.

"C'mon—surely there's something better to do during Golden Week."

""Such as?""

They're in perfect unison.

I actually couldn't come up with an alternative.

"See, Mana's saying she's coming even if her bubby's not," Fushimi said as she showed me her phone's screen.

Mana had indeed pulled the rug out from under me. Now I couldn't use her as a means to thwart their plans.

She doesn't even know Shinohara…but I guess that wouldn't faze her. Her social prowess is too high.

"Ryou, do you have any past traumatic experiences with barbecue or something?"

"Uh, no."

The closest thing to it I'd experienced was a summer party when I was a kid.

"We had one during third year back in grade school, remember? That was fun. We swam in the pool, had barbecue, played with fireworks," Fushimi said while counting each event with her fingers.

"…I also want fireworks."

"Yeah, let's."

"We'll make some good memories."

"Golden Week memories."

""Let's do it!""

They joined hands with scorching enthusiasm. There was no stopping them.

"You too, Ryou." Fushimi held out her other hand, grinning with all her might. Torigoe did the same, asking me to join their circle.

"Fine." I reluctantly accepted.

"Don't be that way. I'm sure you'll enjoy it the most out of us."

"Nah."

"Yeah, Takamori's pretending to be a stick-in-the-mud."

"I will never let barbecue into my heart. Ever."

"Yup, he's gonna love it."

"Yeah."

We didn't go back to studying after that—we started talking about where it would be and what food to bring. This certainly was more fun than studying, so I listened to the conversation while occasionally nodding in agreement or giving my opinion.

"Fushimi, you don't have to worry about your classes?"

"Huh? Oh, no, it's fine."

Fushimi already knew Torigoe knew.

"Actually, we'll have a live performance on the last day of the holidays. I'll be showing up just for a bit," she said with a bashful smile. She added that she was currently rehearsing for it.

"What's the story about?" Torigoe eagerly asked.

Fushimi explained, then told us that she'd be participating in only one of the multiple performances the troupe would do. There were two other people cast for the same role, and they'd take turns on different days. The troupe had many alumni from her school, so she had an opportunity to get an interview for joining. The story was a modern, original play, and her role was as the daughter of the protagonist, a woman in her thirties.

"I don't have many lines, but the character's supposed to be in middle school. Won't that feel weird? I mean, I'm almost halfway through high school."

Torigoe glanced at Fushimi, then tilted her head. "You think? Nah, you'll be fine."

…You just looked at her chest, didn't you?

"Good to hear." Fushimi flashed a pure smile.

"Break a leg."

"Thank you."

Torigoe then called Shinohara, who decided to come to us to talk about our plans.

*　　*　　*

Shinohara joined us at a park nearby, we sat at the empty wooden table in the gazebo.

"Why barbecue?"

Shinohara seemed dumbfounded and thought there were better options, but she did agree.

"My sister will be coming, too; is that okay?"

"Oh, Mana? Yeah."

You know her?

"You seem surprised. Truth be told, I have a brother her age and very frequently hear about her. Rumors of this Takamori *gyaru*."

Yeah, she's hard to miss, in more ways than one.

We kept making our plans until the lights came on, alerting us of our now-dark surroundings. We made a group chat with all five of us to talk details and then went our own ways.

"I can't wait…," Fushimi said with an expression of pure bliss on our way home.

"It's already worth doing this, seeing you so excited about it."

"The truth is, I wanted to do this ever since I became friends with Torigoe."

So that's why you were so gung-ho about it.

Fushimi told me everything there was to tell about her plans, then out of nowhere asked me, "Ryou, don't you think you'd enjoy it, too?"

"Acting? No, thank you."

"I think you could really get into it."

"If I did get into acting, I'd prefer being backstage."

"…You could. There's lots of backstage work. Plays are not just about the actors."

She was taking this surprisingly seriously.

"I said 'if.' I have no intention of actually doing it."

"Oh." But Fushimi was not dissuaded. "You know, not everyone in the cast is super good-looking, despite what you may think. Some people shine brightest in supporting roles."

She really, really wanted me to join her in that path.

"You don't even have to get super into it. There are tons of newbies, too."

She glanced at me, probably thinking she was being subtle about it.

"Fine, fine. I'll think about it."

"Yes! I hope you do!" Her smile was dazzling. "If you let yourself, you'll enjoy it. Mark my words." Then she shifted back into a more serious manner. "I just started six months ago, so it's still hard. I have trouble getting things right, but when I do, it feels so good. There's nothing like it."

There she goes again, talking like a manga protagonist.

It was obvious she was the protagonist of her own story. As for my own, I still didn't know. But likely, for now, my protagonist was her.

First day of Golden Week came, and we went to a camping spot deep in the mountains.

"Bubby, look! Crabs! Look!"

Mana crouched beside the mountain stream, pointing excitedly.

"Please don't embarrass me."

What are you, five? Well, she is the youngest in this group.

By the way, the oldest person there was Mr. Tsunehisa. My mom was second place. Kids weren't allowed to come here all by ourselves, so we held the barbecue accompanied by the Fushimi and Takamori guardians, who drove us there.

"Mana's so cute…" Fushimi sighed in bliss.

Mr. Tsunehisa and I did the heavy lifting while the others unloaded the food.

"Ryou, want to light the coals with me?" he asked.

"Sure."

The camping spot had water and other facilities and tools right by for use.

"Mana, you're the best at this, so stop playing with the crabs and come help." My mom called for her after having a smoke.

"Ahem." Fushimi cleared her throat. "Well then, Dad and Ryou will be starting the fire. I'll go get cooking."

She rolled up her sleeves with a huge smirk on her face. Torigoe grabbed her shoulder with a grimace.

"Fushimi, you do something else. We have enough cooks in the kitchen."

"Y-you sure?"

Mana stopped messing with the crabs and nodded with a serious expression.

Yeah, we can't have the full-pumpkin alchemist turning everything into hot garbage. Our resources are limited.

"...And you'll just be sitting there, Shinohara?"

"Don't worry about me. I'll be fanning you, Takaryou."

"At least fan the fire instead..."

Shinohara sat next to me and started fanning me. The cool breeze felt really good.

I turned to look at the kitchen and saw Fushimi cleaning the wire mesh.

"It's been since grade school that Hina last hung out with someone like this," Mr. Tsunehisa commented in a low voice.

I'd been hanging out with her pretty frequently way back when and more recently, but I guessed I didn't count as *"someone."*

The fire spread throughout the coals, lighting them up in orange as the sparks crackled.

"Here's the mesh." Fushimi placed the now-clean mesh on the grill.

The fashion police had supervised her light outfit and cap, and her hair was tied up in a ponytail.

"She even said she couldn't sleep last night," Mr. Tsunehisa said, watching Fushimi.

"Are you…? C'mon—you're not in grade school anymore…"

"N-no, it's not that. I just stayed up so late getting stuff ready…"

Mana approached us, holding a bowl with cut-up ingredients in it.

"As if the same didn't happen to you, Bubby."

"No, it didn't. It's not like I was too excited to sleep. I just have insomnia."

"Yeah, right." She giggled as she went back to the kitchen.

"You're such a kid." Shinohara smirked at me.

"Shut up, edgelord. Go follow the path of your fate or something."

"I'm cured now! I'm normal!" She hit me again and again with her fan.

"Huh? …Aren't you guys so friendly now?" Fushimi asked, puzzled.

"No, we aren't."

"Not like Takaryou would ever accept that; he's so stubborn and coy."

"Who you calling coy?!"

"Our next stop is Meat Station, Meat Station…," Mr. Tsunehisa announced as he stood up to go check the cooler.

"We could've dated for much longer if you had just been honest and told me you liked me back then!" She poked me with her fan, a devious smile on her face.

"Stop it. We didn't even date."

You said it yourself—it was just a dare.

"Huh? What are you talking about?" Fushimi asked, bewildered.

Right, I haven't told her yet.

"Shinohara asked me out in second year of middle school."

"Oh, I see." She stood up. "I'm going to the restroom."

Her face was hidden by the cap, but she seemed sad.

Shinohara's expression turned serious. "Hey, didn't you tell her?"

"Do I need to tell her everything?"

"Ugh… For crying out loud… I should've been more careful." She flung her head back. "Oh, dear God up in the heavens. Please let today's barbecue poison this guy and end his life."

"What in the hell are you asking right now? Shut up."

Shinohara sighed a sigh so heavy, I worried her soul might've left her body along with it.

"I didn't tell her, but since it was just a dare, why does it matter?"

"It wasn't…a dare."

Huh?

I stared at her. She fanned me without turning my way.

"I'm sorry… I just went with what you said when you brought it up and let you draw your own crazy conclusions. But it's not true."

"It isn't…?"

"Don't worry about me anymore. Go look for her."

"But she said she went to the restroom."

"She didn't."

But what if she did?

Shinohara didn't care about my doubts. "I think I could get along with her, and I don't want her to hate me now," she whispered. "I thought she already knew, so I was just joking around. I apologize for that."

"But if it wasn't a dare, then…"

"Oh, sh-shut it. It was three years ago."

She poked me with her elbow again and again until I stood up to go look for Fushimi. I first went to the restroom to wait for her outside, but it didn't seem like she was there. No one was.

Where are you, Fushimi?

I returned to the stream where Mana was playing and followed it up to a tiny waterfall. There, I saw a girl in a cap sitting below the stone steps. I walked toward her when suddenly, she yelled at me.

"Ryou, you asshoooooooole!"

The sound of the waterfall dampened its volume, but I was close enough to hear it.

"You said you'd never kissed anybody, you liaaaaaaaar!"

Oh, but I haven't. Seriously.

"And I'm sure you already did all sorts of dirty things with her! You piiiiiiiiig!"

You think you can slander me just because you believe no one can hear?

"Gaaaahhhh!" she screamed as she grabbed a big stone with both hands and threw it toward the waterfall.

Where's all that power coming from in those thin arms?

"Heeey, Fushimiii! Are you theeere?"

"Ryou, you sleaze... Huh?" Fushimi immediately dropped the second rock she was about to throw. "Wh-what's the matter, Ryou?"

No, you can't just put on a straight face now. I already saw your gorilla-like strength.

"I want to explain something. It seems you're misunderstanding."

"What?"

I sat on the stone steps and explained everything that had happened with Shinohara. She sat down beside me and listened carefully.

"...Just three days?"

"Yes. She said, 'Can't do it,' and dumped me right away. So...we haven't kissed. And definitely not anything more. We didn't even hold hands or go back home together."

"Doubt."

"Excuse me?"

"You did go back home with her one time. Just the two of you," she said, now in hamster bomb mode.

"No waaay..."

"Yes way. I know it."

"How do you know?"

"I saw you. I was in shock, since you broke one of our promises."

©Fly

What promise? When did I even promise that? There was no safe way of asking that then, so I ignored the issue.

"Well, whatever. It was just three days, so it all ended before we could even get close."

"I see…," she said, playing with a rock by her feet. Her voice dropped to barely a whisper. "If you really haven't kissed anyone yet…I want your first…to be with me…"

She put her hand on mine. My heart almost jumped out of my chest, beating faster and faster.

Thump, thump-thump, thump…

I felt her cold fingers start to warm up. She pouted ever so slightly and raised her chin. I had no clear recollection of this, but I bet I had so easily promised we'd share our first kiss because I liked her when we were little. I gulped.

R-really? I can do it? Seriously?

"Bubby?"

That voice brought us back to reality, and we swiftly jumped apart. Our years together had us in complete synchrony for this sort of stuff.

"Oh, there you are! Why are you slacking off? Whoa, holy cow! There's a waterfall there!" Mana exclaimed in wonder, her eyes sparkling.

"L-let's go."

"Y-yeah…"

Things were still awkward between us. I wouldn't be able to look straight at her for a good while. The memory of her expression then had my heart beating faster.

"You were flirting with Hina, weren't you?" Mana grinned.

"N-n-no-no, no," I replied.

I wasn't sure that counted as *"flirting,"* but it was pretty close. She'd probably said it as a joke, but it hit too close to home.

"…"

Mana looked at me, then at Fushimi, then back at me.

"…No way—you were making out in the woods?"

"N-no, Mana! We were just, um… Ryou was helping me get rid of something that got in my eye."

That's such a clichéd excuse!

"Oh, really?"

She bought it!

"Yeah, that was it."

"You should've told me, Hina. I could've lent you a mirror," said Mana.

She even proposed an alternate solution…

"Y-yeah, thank you!" Not even the actor-in-training could give a convincing performance this time.

"If Tori had seen you two… Oh."

"You found them?" Torigoe asked, soaked in sweat and out of breath.

"…You're too desperate, Tori."

"Wh-why do you care?"

"You were worried, weren't you? In more ways than one."

"I don't like cheeky girls like you, little miss."

"Oh, you do." Mana poked Torigoe with her finger.

Torigoe then noticed us and observed us carefully.

"…"

"Torigoe, is everything ready?" Fushimi asked as cheerily as she could.

"Yeah, I think it's all done," she replied.

"Let's go, then," Fushimi said, leading the way.

"Bubby, you were doing sexy stuff, weren't you?"

"I'm telling you, *no.*"

"Don't forget to zip up again."

"I never unzipped."

My fly was tightly closed, thank you. I hadn't even gone to the bathroom since we got there.

"Dammit, you never fall for these things. Boooring."

"I already know all your tricks."

"Play along for once!" My little sister threw a hissy fit. "So, were you about to kiss?"

"…You're too cheeky for your own good."

"Oooh, so I ruined the mood, huh. Hee-hee-hee, truth be told, your first kiss was with me." She did a peace sign.

"Seriously?"

"Yes, I stole a kiss from my sleeping beauty. ♡ Hee-hee-hee."

"…When exactly?"

Not that it would count with her. It also depended on how old we were, and I hadn't even been conscious in the first place.

"Tori was really anxious, y'know? Besides, a boy and a girl just up and disappearing in the middle of a barbecue is like a neon sign saying something is going on out there."

I really wasn't expecting her to get so desperate, though. Like, gasping-and-covered-in-sweat desperate.

The meat and vegetables were already getting cooked on the mesh by the time we got back. My mom was tending the grill as she chatted. She grabbed some meat with tongs and put it on a plate for me. This was good meat—Mr. Tsunehisa had probably splurged on it. It was incredible.

A heavy cloud had settled around Torigoe and Fushimi, seated next to each other. Shinohara knew the reason, so she tried to get them talking.

Mana sighed. "Geez… You're such a dummy, Bubby…"

"Hey, stop dissing me out of nowhere."

After a while, the girls declared they were full and immediately went to get the sweets they bought at the convenience store out from the cooler.

Didn't you just say you were full?

Shortly after, I was full as well.

"There's a waterfall over there! Let's all go together," Mana said, and the three of them left.

I wasn't included. I stared at them, waiting for an invitation, but no luck. I had to stay behind, listening to my mom and Mr. Tsunehisa chat about the neighborhood. They mentioned a neighbor from a house five minutes from ours. I immediately got bored and decided to go join the girls at the waterfall, where I found two girls firmly grabbing each other—Shinohara and Mana.

"What are you two doing?"

"Sumo!" Fushimi answered.

"Sumo…?"

Sumo, huh. I see…

No… I don't get it. What the hell?!

"Byagh?!" Mana squealed like a frog getting crushed as she got thrown into the stream. It was shallow enough that she stood up right away.

"Shino, you're so strong!"

"Mii, the glasses girl is supposed to lose in this sort of thing. You're supposed to fall down and lose your glasses. Go on."

"What? No."

I looked closely and noticed Fushimi and Torigoe were also soaking wet. So they'd gotten the same treatment as Mana.

"Next. Hina versus Tori."

Suddenly, the chill vibes evaporated into high tension.

"I won't lose, Torigoe."

"Do your best. I don't plan on losing, either."

They grabbed each other at the same time. They weren't moving at all, but I could tell they were both pushing hard. Mana got tired of cheering after a while and approached them.

"You're taking too long." Then she pushed them both into the stream.

"Eeeek?!"

"Waaah!"

Mana clapped as she watched them fall; then Shinohara pushed her down, too.

I'm getting cold just watching them.

"Heeey!"

"Shinohara, you should fall down here, too. It's more fun that way."

"No way. I don't want to get wet."

C'mon, Shinohara, go along with it.

"What are you all doing? How're you planning on drying yourselves?"

You didn't bring a change of clothes, did you? Geez.

I got closer to them.

Good grief. What a bunch of kids.

"We'll dry. It's sunny today."

"Well, I hope you do."

Fushimi and Torigoe seemed somehow relieved.

" … "

My eyes met Fushimi's, then Torigoe's. You might expect this to lead to some awkward scene where their underwear showed through their clothes or something—but instead, they looked at each other, then at me.

Why am I suddenly imagining kids planning a prank…?

They both ran up to me, then grabbed my arms.

Oh crap—

"Hey, wait a sec… Stop it!"

""Off you go!""

They pushed me full force into the stream.

"Bwah?! Oh God, it's so cold!" I yelled.

Mana cackled.

I thought Shinohara at least would worry about me, but she was also giggling.

"You bunch of—!"

"We won't get in trouble if everyone's wet, you know?"

Fushimi and Torigoe laughed.

"Which means…"

Everyone turned to look at Shinohara.

"N-no! Hey! This is bullying!"

"Mii, don't worry. Maybe falling in will give you superpowers."

"At least put some thought into the lore!"

Shinohara shook her head as hard as she could, but she couldn't resist the three of them and splooshed down right beside me.

After she checked that her glasses were all right, we got up to the shore. We had no towels or anything we could use to dry off with, so we just settled down in the sunshine.

"So…how did this happen, again?"

"Mana. She was like, 'You should sumo wrestle!'"

"Guess we all got caught up in the moment."

"Hey, I didn't know we'd end up in the water!"

Perhaps Mana did it out of concern for them, so that the barbecue wouldn't end on an awkward note.

"I'm soaked, but that was fun."

""""Yeah.""""""

The sky was so blue. The early-summer sun was brighter than expected—our clothes would dry before we knew it.

Despite how warm the sunlight was, it was only the start of May, a fact that became obvious by how soon the sun set. The mountains quickly got colder and colder.

Mana made some *yakisoba* with the leftover meat and veggies for dinner. Afterward, we played with sparklers, as Torigoe had requested. Mom started lighting them for us with the included candle.

"Me first!" Mana exclaimed, holding her sparkler to the fire. The light spread as it fully ignited. "So pretty!" She squealed like a little girl.

Torigoe ignited hers as well.

"Good thing they work even if they're the cheapest I could find."

"Shii, don't say those things. You're ruining the fun." The sparks illuminated Shinohara's expression of exasperation.

"I just said the truth."

"Don't worry, girls. Just call it 'cost-effective,'" Fushimi said.

"Bubby, here, I'll light yours."

"Thanks."

The smell of smoke and powder was the smell of summer.

Mine gave off a pea-green-colored light. It had been so long since I last did this; it was hard to take my eyes off it.

After going through most of the usual types, we finally changed to the fragile *senko hanabi* sparklers.

The orange sphere at the tip crackled audibly as the sparks sprinkled off it.

"Ryou, let's see whose lasts longer."

"Oh, sure."

Fushimi crouched down beside me, and we stared at the sparklers dangling from our hands.

"Why are these always left for last?" I asked.

"Because they're a bit sad, maybe?"

"I guess I can see that."

"I think they're so we can have some time to accept that it's over. You can't run around with these or shake them all over."

"So it's a more mature kind of firework."

"You're supposed to reflect on the day. Savor the aftertaste, you know?"

My sparkler's tip was getting smaller and smaller.

"Hi-ya!" Fushimi yelled and stuck her tip against mine.

"What happened to trying to outlast me?"

"I don't mind losing." Fushimi laughed, her sparkler still not leaving mine. "It's stuck."

"You stuck it."

"It's fine; it's fine."

Mana started loudly going on about taking pictures of the fireworks, and Torigoe and Shinohara joined her.

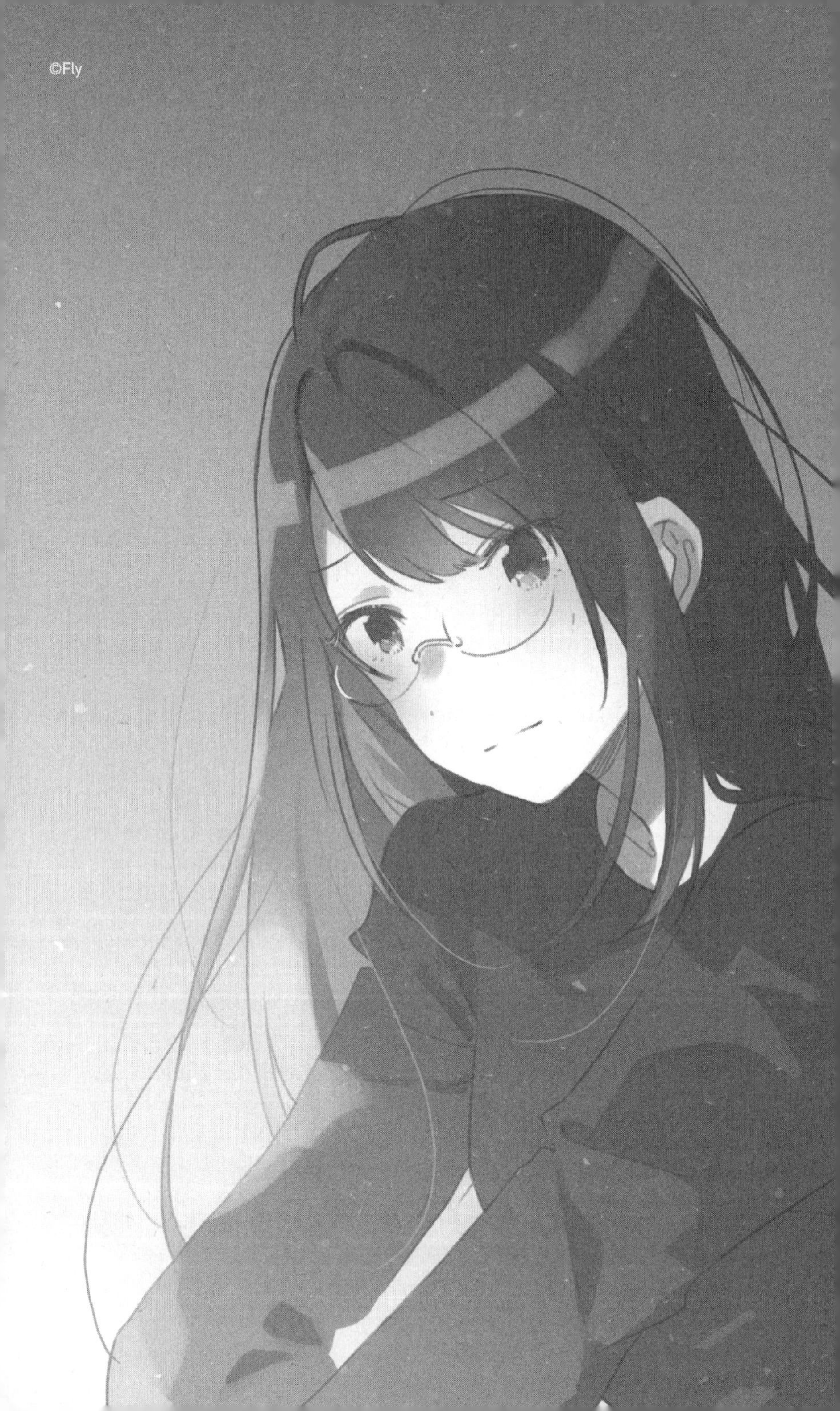
©Fly

There was a gust of wind, and our joined sparkler tips dropped to the ground. The loss of the only light source made the night feel especially dark. She grabbed the hand I'd been holding the sparkler with, and as I turned to ask why, her lips touched mine. It took me a few moments to realize what had happened.

While I was still frozen in time, Fushimi shyly whispered, "I did it." The darkness didn't let me see her face then.

Fushimi stood up and walked over to Mana and the other girls before I could say anything.

"I want to take some photos, too!"

"Hina, look at this! Isn't it so pretty?! So aesthetic?!"

I felt as though the girls' voices were getting farther and farther away.

Was that an accident? Did she just bump into me?

"But she said, 'I did it…'"

I touched my lips again, then thought back to what almost happened before the barbecue.

"…"

We probably would've kissed had Mana not arrived. So that meant Fushimi was already ready to do it?

We're technically alone together here, but they were right over there. What if they saw us? Be more careful.

"…She's bolder than I thought…"

The girls squealed as they played with their sparklers, phones in hand.

"…"

I couldn't get it out of my mind—the sight of her face so close to mine or the touch of her lips.

"I might be dreaming about this tonight."

In fact, it would feel more realistic if I were already in a dream.

I tossed my sparkler into the small bucket full of water. The other expended sticks jutted out of the bucket like a confused sea anemone.

Torigoe, Shinohara, and I went to the main hall of the community center.

I wondered how many spectators could fit in here. About four hundred?

Our reserved seats were at the center of the hall.

"It's bigger than I expected," Torigoe said as she took the seat beside mine, scanning around.

"The community theater can hold up to four hundred and fifty people. It's the biggest one around here," Shinohara explained while looking at her pamphlet. She sat at Torigoe's other side.

Stop acting like you know it all when you're just reading what it says there.

"I've never gone to see a play. I'm pretty excited."

"Me too," I replied.

We'd come to watch Fushimi onstage. She got the tickets for us, so we were able to watch it for free. Regular price was 1,500 yen for high school students, so about the same as a movie ticket. Not especially expensive, but who could ever say no to free stuff?

"It's the kind of thing you rarely come see unless there are special circumstances, like now."

"...Now I'm the one getting nervous."

Spectators started arriving, and 80 percent of the seats were full twenty minutes before showtime.

"I'll be acting here, so please come!"

Fushimi had been red when she gave me the ticket.

...Truth be told, I was expecting something shabbier. I didn't even know about the community troupe, so I'd just assumed they were volunteers doing small plays here and there.

"This is no kids' play, huh?"

"Apparently, the director is pretty well-known in the industry," Torigoe whispered.

The director was pretty famous; there were a whole bunch of plays listed under the photo in the pamphlet. He also did the screenplay this time around.

I barely knew the title of *Romeo and Juliet*, so I was blank on the listed plays.

Fushimi has been practicing all this time, while I was just messing around in my house, huh?

"Oh, this dude was born here," Shinohara told us after looking him up on her phone.

"What if Fushimi becomes a star after this play?"

"Nah, that never happens in real life."

Although she certainly had the power to steal the spotlight. She had what it took to get famous.

"I bet she could," Torigoe said in a firm tone.

Fushimi basically had her career laid out for her. She was so beautiful, ten people out of ten would turn her way—perfect for an acting role. And there she was, about to get onstage.

"I guess Fushimi has her life set on easy mode."

"I wonder about that. But she certainly has it easier than I do."

"What are you two jealous for?"

I tried to reply that that wasn't it when the lights slowly faded out and the curtain started rising.

There was no need for detailed world building, since it was set in modern times. The protagonist and her husband started talking in a panic. She had just killed someone and needed his help covering up the crime.

So it was a suspense story that touched on social issues. Nothing happy or cheery.

As the story went on, we learned the victim was the woman's daughter. Fushimi made her appearance in a flashback scene, so at least she wasn't just a corpse. She was wearing a typical middle school sailor uniform that looked great on her.

Fushimi gave her performance with an elegant, clear voice that you usually wouldn't hear from her. I'd never seen this side of her, actually. She was shining like a star, and I didn't think it was because of the spotlight on her or her special makeup.

Flashbacks were interspersed throughout the story, showing Fushimi's character from before she died and slowly revealing the mystery. The structure sucked you right in; before you knew it, you were invested.

…Actually, she's no side character. She's pretty crucial to the story!

By the end, the motive and method of the murder connected it to the intro scene. That was the last scene. There was no bigger plot twist or comeuppance; you just got the catharsis of knowing why.

Applause burst as the curtain fell; then Fushimi and the other actors gathered for the final bow. The clapping only increased until the actors went backstage, and the lights of the theater came back on.

"…"

"…"

Both girls were in awe.

"That was…really good," I said. They both nodded.

"She's been at this for half a year?"

"Yeah."

I couldn't tell good acting from bad acting, but considering she didn't get in the way of the story, I assumed she did well enough.

"It's incredible she got chosen for this. She told me it was by pure chance, but I don't know."

It was as if Fushimi were flying, while everyone else had to walk. But I bet she was working hard, just where no one could see it.

It also didn't seem like her first play. If it was, she would've told me so when she gave me the ticket.

We left the hall, and then I received a text from Fushimi.

There's like a café inside, wait for me there.

I relayed the message to the other two, and we waited for her at the café inside the building.

"H-how was it?"

"Fushimi, you're so good. It was amazing," Torigoe said, delivering her impressions with an almost childlike bluntness.

Shinohara nodded. "The story was very interesting, too."

"Glad to hear." Fushimi glanced at me, since I still hadn't said anything.

Torigoe and Shinohara, sitting on either side of me, simultaneously jabbed me with their elbows.

"Um… Well, I've never seen this side of you. You were cool up there."

"Hee-hee. Not cool getting killed, though."

She excitedly gave us the rundown on all the backstage drama, and we listened attentively. Then she said they had a short lunch break before they needed to prepare for the afternoon showing.

"Thanks for coming. See you!" Fushimi waved with a smile as she left.

I was honestly impressed. She was acting alongside those adults like a professional. Maybe she would really become a star. And that star had kissed me…

"It starts to feel like we're living in different worlds," Torigoe muttered.

That was when I understood everything. Yes, I thought Fushimi was amazing, and I had mad respect for her, but Torigoe was right. That was the strange feeling I'd started having recently. The childhood friend I'd played with since I was little was slowly becoming someone I didn't know.

I got a call from Fushimi that night, while I was lazing around in my room.

She sounded really happy. Her costars, and even Mr. Kudo—the play's director—had praised her performance.

"Mr. Kudo never keeps anything to himself. He said they didn't let him do what he wanted in Tokyo, so he came back to his hometown to do it."

That was how a community troupe got an accomplished director for their play. Fushimi was telling me all about that dark side of the industry people generally don't want to hear, like how getting a big corporate sponsor can stifle your creativity.

"Ryou, can we meet right now?"

"Fine by me." I looked at the clock; it was already past ten. "I mean, no problem for me, but what about you? Don't you have a curfew?"

I remembered Mr. Tsunehisa once saying she shouldn't be out so late.

"It's fine. No one will know I'm gone."

I hadn't seen him at the theater, now that I thought about it. Maybe there were special seats elsewhere, and he was there.

I grabbed my phone and wallet and headed for the entrance.

"Bubby, where are you going?" Mana asked. She'd already taken a bath, so she had no makeup on.

Bubby thinks you're perfectly cute without makeup, you know?

"Um... I have something to do."

"What would that be?"

"Why do you care?"

"Ah. Hina."

"Maybe, maybe," I replied on my way out. *How does she know?*

I met with Fushimi halfway to her house. I couldn't go back now that she'd seen me, so I suggested we head to the park.

"Sorry for calling you so late."

"It's only ten; it's not that late."

Considering her schedule, it probably was for her.

"I just couldn't sleep once I started thinking about the play."

You really were trying to sleep this early?

We arrived at a park furnished with only a seesaw, some swings, and two benches. They used to look so big back then, but now they felt tiny.

"It gets pretty chilly at night, huh?" Fushimi scooted closer to me once we sat down.

We could talk about so many things: the midterms coming up the following week, Torigoe or Shinohara...but we couldn't share all of it. I stayed away from that one topic, but I felt like that was probably what she wanted to talk about.

"I still have a long ways to go, but it made me realize again how fun acting is."

"I see."

"Oh," "really," and "I see" were the only three things I could say.

"The barbecue was so fun, too! And the fireworks. Let's do it again next year," Fushimi said, looking up to the sky as though reminiscing about the distant past. I think she was noticing my lackluster reactions.

"...Sorry I can't keep up with what you really want to talk about."

"No, I'm happy with you just listening."

I finally understood why people in the same club always hung out together.

"Did you have fun at the barbecue, Ryou?"

"Yeah, it wasn't bad."

Was it best to not say anything about what had happened during the fireworks?

Thinking back, Fushimi must have been looking for a way to bring it up.

"What's wrong?" she asked.

"Uh, no, nothing." I had subconsciously started staring at her lips.

"Is that so?" Fushimi was calm as always, on the other hand. She didn't seem the least bit embarrassed or self-conscious. "Oh, but to make it clear, I'm not used to that, you know?"

"Used to what?"

"K-kissing…"

"Kissing?"

"Y-yeah… I had to, uh, run a lot of scenarios."

You practiced for that?

"That one was scenario L."

"Just how many did you simulate?"

"Torigoe and the others didn't notice, did they?"

"I hope not."

They could also just be keeping quiet about it. Not like they had to tell us or anything.

"…You won't try and kiss me yourself, Ryou?"

"Huh?"

"N-nothing, sorry." She turned her face away and apologized quietly. "I mean, like, just one…as a reward for my work today…"

"Hey. You're only supposed to do that after you start dating… Same for what you did at the barbecue, too. Just so you know."

"Then let's go out."

"You can't just say it like that! C'mon."

"Wait. If we have to do it after we start dating, then does that mean we will eventually?" She turned my way, her eyes shining brightly.

"Stop trying to mess with my words. I didn't mean it like that… I just still don't understand a lot of things."

"But you dated Shinohara, right? What's the holdup?" She looked at me with discontent.

"That…didn't happen because I liked her or anything…"

"Then you shouldn't have accepted, huh? Aren't you contradicting yourself, huh? Huh?"

Dammit, she's totally right. Can't argue with that.

But I was also happy about it.

Fushimi immediately brightened and started giggling.

"Sorry, that was mean."

"You little…"

"Let me tease you just a bit, okay? I've rejected all of them, by the way. Aaaall of them."

Truly, she had a will of steel. Plenty of people had asked her out—classmates, older guys, younger guys, even guys from other schools, and girls from time to time—and she had told every single one of them no.

"That doesn't have anything to do with me. It's your own decision."

"Yeah, of course. After all, I was in love. Unrequited love. I had to keep saying no." She fluttered her feet, then stared right at me and asked, "…Tell me, is that love still unrequited?"

She was so close. I could feel my face turning red. I leaned backward to regain some distance.

"W-wait, calm down. Why are you so pushy today?"

"Because no one's around."

Is that any reason?

"I felt like I showed you how cool and awesome I was. I thought that would have you falling for me."

"I am not. What do you take me for, a girls' manga heroine?"

Fushimi laughed out loud. "Nice comeback."

Thanks. Now shut up.

Before I knew it, it was almost midnight. I decided it was time to go back home, so I offered to see her off.

She started poking my fingers.

"?"

"..."

She stared at me, and I wondered what she could possibly want to say, when she grabbed my hand. The poking was just the warm-up.

"You can brush me off if you hate it. But if you don't mind—even if you don't particularly like it—then let's do this."

So anything besides hating it meant that I had to keep holding her hand, and she was leaving that decision up to me. No fair.

"I won't go anywhere so long as you're by my side. So hold me tight."

We both naturally unlocked hands in front of her house.

"Fushimi...you think you'll be a famous actress?"

"Even if I get my big break, I'll come back home—to you. For sure."

She stayed there outside, fidgety. I wondered why she didn't go inside.

"Listen...I will come back. So please love me?"

With that, she fled into her house.

◆Shizuka Torigoe◆

Perhaps it wasn't anything special from their point of view.

I'd seen Fushimi kiss Takamori after our barbecue, when we were playing with sparklers. At first I thought she was whispering in his ear, but they were too close for that.

Fushimi was in love with Takamori. Meanwhile, he saw her as a childhood friend, a beautiful girl more special to him than others. So it wasn't anything special *for them.*

Wouldn't you find that special person hard to manage? I typed, lying on my bed.

She wasn't a normal girl. She got everyone's attention and had everyone spreading rumors about her.

"Is she really not dating Takamori?"

"Man, she's always so cute."

"Someone asked her out again."

Everyone was always paying attention to each and every movement of the school's star. And if they started dating, Takamori would join her at the center of attention. Naturally. This sort of romance was perfect fuel for the gossipy girls.

Do you think you could have a normal romance with such a special girl, Takamori? I finished typing, then immediately deleted it all.

I was jealous of my friend again. God, this sucked.

Just date already. 'Cause it'll be hard.

"…"

He probably wasn't even conscious of the surroundings, considering how thick his skull was. But I didn't want him to go on like that. It would be hard for me. I didn't want to become the kind of person who would wish misfortune on her friend or the boy she liked.

Fushimi was too sweet for her own good, and mine, too. If only she had a dark side, it'd be so much easier to hope for her demise.

"Not keeping that." I deleted what I'd just typed.

I felt a bit relieved after typing out the words and seeing them. Perhaps it wouldn't be so bad keeping them, but I was sure I'd just get grumpy again once I read them later. It was better for my mental health to delete them.

I want a kiss, too.

I wondered how that had felt. I wondered if that was their first. How many times had they done that before?

"…"

I subconsciously touched my lips with my index finger. I grabbed the plushie beside my pillow and gave it a soft kiss. My heart didn't beat faster, and the only thing I felt on my lips was the fabric. As expected, it did nothing for me.

"She didn't have to do it right then…"

Was she just oblivious? Or had she lost her mind?

I honestly felt like Fushimi was too much for Takamori.

Did he really want to go see her performance?

He probably didn't. He didn't seem like he was forcing himself to do it, but he wasn't exactly having the time of his life, even if the play itself was great.

Just as Mii told me right before the play, maybe I was just jealous. Jealous that Fushimi seemed to get whatever she wanted and do whatever she wanted. And the only thing that didn't go her way was Takamori.

He didn't seem happy at all when we found out she was going to the actors' school. I knew the feeling. I started wondering where I was heading, what I should do. It was like when someone tells you to draw something, anything, on a pure-white canvas. Like someone had told me to move in whatever direction I wanted when all I could see was the sea and the sky.

Not everyone could act out the textbook role of a high schooler full of dreams. In fact, there were probably way fewer people who did have a dream, and even fewer who could and did put in the effort to achieve it. And that went for anyone, not just high schoolers.

I'm sure I can understand how you feel, Takamori.

My monologue started getting cringy, like a stalker character in a girls' manga. I was getting embarrassed just reading it, so I deleted it. But in the end, it was all how I really felt.

Don't you think so, Takamori? Isn't Fushimi too bright for us?

You can't get too close to the sun.

And you can't look directly at it.

Yet, there was no distance between them at all. From what I could tell, I was sure they had kissed multiple times before. They should just start dating, in that case. Then break up at a moderate distance. I didn't have to be Takamori's first.

I would come in and heal his wounds after he'd flown too close to the sun. I didn't have just one chance and done; this outcome was perfectly fine.

I was getting disgusted at myself for thinking so selfishly, calculatingly. But please understand. What else could I do when I had to see them so chummy and intimate every single day?

I held my plushie tight, feeling nothing but the lukewarm cloth and cotton.

Everyone in class was calling me *Prez* by the time midterms approached. I'd told them many times before I was only class representative, but no one seemed to care about technicalities. They just liked how *Prez* sounded.

"Class reps, you two round up the papers and bring them over to me later!" Waka, our homeroom teacher, waved at us as she left the classroom.

She'd given us career path survey papers first thing in the morning and said, "It's fine if you don't have any concrete plans, but it's best to think about them now."

"Make sure to think through what you want to be in the future! Will you go on to humanities? Sciences? Public? Private?" Fushimi said. It was a perfect imitation of Waka.

"What're you gonna do, Fushimi?"

"I'll go to college. That's the plan for now."

"Not going to do, you know, that?" I had to know.

"That's another story. We're talking about the bigger picture here, and I can handle both the big and little pics."

I snorted.

I guess she still wants to keep that promise about attending college together. Not that I recall ever making it.

"But what if everything goes too well and you...start starring in TV dramas or movies?"

Fushimi thought for a bit, then grinned. "I'll quit at the height of my popularity. Like at twenty-five or something. I'll announce that I'm going back to my hometown to marry a regular person, then flee Tokyo."

It sounded like she was genuinely dreaming of doing that.

"What a waste."

"It's not a waste!" Still beaming, she stared right at me. "I wonder what kind of person you'll be when you grow up."

"That's what I want to know. Not like I have any big dreams like you," I grumbled and sighed.

She suddenly pinched my cheek. "You've been making this face too much lately."

"You think?"

"Yeah."

I brushed her hand away and prepared for class. "We ordinary people have ordinary problems to think about."

"…I think that's true for anyone."

"I guess." I shrugged.

So she said, but I couldn't even imagine her having any worries of the sort.

"Torigoe, what did you write for the survey?"

It was lunchtime. I finished eating the food Mana had made for me and was then browsing my phone when I asked that.

Torigoe was sitting slightly far away. She finished chewing, then answered, "Public university. Whichever around this area."

"You think you can make it with a single-digit test result in English?"

"English is the only subject I'm not good at."

Meanwhile, I was bad at pretty much all of them.

"But Waka said you should think about what you want to be in the future," I said.

"That's for people who want to learn a trade. Like if you want to become a beautician or if you want to get on a tuna-fishing boat. You wouldn't have to go to university for those. You can just do a vocational school."

Are there vocational schools for fishermen...?

"So you watched that tuna-fishing documentary recently, huh?"

"Anything wrong with that?"

"No, I saw it, too."

Funny coincidence.

"So let's say you get in that public university," she continued. "Then what?"

"I dunno. Ask me a few years later, once I'm there."

"...Okay."

Yeah, not like I knew, either. Who knew what I would become. I'd rather people wait a few years before asking.

I knew what I'd be doing the following year—I'd be in my third year of high school. I'd probably follow everyone else, studying for entrance exams as a vague goal. But I had no idea what would happen the year after. That was only two years away, and I was drawing a blank.

Torigoe then asked me about Fushimi's answer. I told her exactly as she'd told me, and she reacted in a similar way to mine. I stopped halfway through, thinking back on what Fushimi had said that morning about quitting at the peak of her career. I'd brushed it off then, but was that ordinary person she talked about...supposed to be me?

"...Then what? What will Fushimi do if she gets famous?"

"Uh, um... J-just ask her."

"Why are you red all of a sudden?"

"Nothing." I grabbed my empty lunch box and got away from the physics room as fast as I could.

Is Fushimi really thinking that?

"Even though we're not dating...?"

"What're you muttering about?"

"Wha—?!" I jumped at the voice calling me from behind, then turned around to find Waka there.

"How're the surveys going?"

"Um, yeah, we're getting some here and there…"

"Don't forget to fill yours out, too. You could be a florist or a pastry chef for all I care, but do it."

What am I, a little girl?

"Oh, but don't write down 'livestreamer,' okay? I don't care if you say you can make enough money from that; I don't want anything that would make for a long meeting session with your parents."

"O…kay?" I replied.

She then made an expression I wasn't expecting. "Takamori, you're really putting thought into this, aren't you? Even though you're not so smart?"

"How could you tell?"

…And why are you dissing me in the process? I mean, you're not wrong, but…

"You're the type to write whatever answer comes to mind, wrong or not, but you're being uncharacteristically vague. It's fine. Go on, give your future some real thought."

Waka slapped my shoulder a couple of times, then left. Just after she turned the corner, she peeked at me again.

"My recommendation is some kind of government-paid job. That's always your best bet if you don't know what to do. Teachers and parents alike will always feel safe hearing that, even if you're not serious. We won't have any problems during the meeting that way. I'm glad I did it myself. Being a teacher is pretty easy," she said before finally leaving.

I told Fushimi just that on our way home.

"I'll get a government job."

"Sounds good," she said. "But do you really want to?"

"How could you tell?"

"Just a gut feeling."

Her smile was wide and happy about successfully seeing through my lies.

"The truth is, I don't want to become anything."

"Uh-oh, there it is…the darkness of modern life." She made an *oops* face. "Ryou, you just have to be yourself."

"And what does that mean?" I nearly chuckled.

Still, that almost sounded deep. Deep to me, if to no one else, anyway.

"Let's study."

Torigoe came to my house early in the morning one Saturday, while Fushimi had her lesson. I hurriedly changed out of my pajamas, then went to receive her at the entrance while my brain was still struggling to wake up.

"Um… Torigoe, do you have any idea what time it is?"

"Not as early as you think. It's around the time you'd have to get going to school."

"Yes, but it's the weekend. Please."

It was eight in the morning. Which meant I still had two hours of sleep for my usual schedule.

She'd proposed the idea the day before, saying she'd get there during the morning. I accepted, thinking that meant, like, around ten.

"It's eight o'clock. That's morning."

"I mean, yes, technically."

I let her in. She was wearing perfectly normal casual clothes, the ones any sane high school girl would wear…unlike Fushimi's usual style.

"…What are you staring at me for?"

"Oh, nothing… Mana made breakfast—want some?"

"Your sis really is like your mom, huh?"

She accepted the offer, so I took her to the dining room.

"Tori, what's the matter today?" Mana seemed excited.

"We're studying. Takamori's dumb, don't you think? He needs it."

"C'mon—stop it."

Hey, I just woke up. I don't need this.

"Yeah. Take good care of him; he really is dumb. In multiple ways."

"You too?"

Breakfast was Japanese-style that day: rolled omelet, grilled fish, white rice, pickled daikon, and miso soup.

"Ah, I have to go in a bit! Mama won't be home until the evening, so you two will be all alone here together."

"You don't have to warn us so explicitly," Torigoe said after taking a bite of the daikon.

"I have to, or Bubby won't notice."

"Yeah, you're right."

What are you two talking about?

We finished breakfast, and I led Torigoe to my room on the second floor. That was when I realized it was the first time I was letting a girl who wasn't Fushimi or Mana into my room.

It's all tidied up, right?

I gave her a cushion so she could sit at the low table.

"Will this really work without Fushimi?"

That had been the first thing I thought the day before, when Torigoe brought it up.

"It's fine. I already asked her what to do."

She showed me the proof on her phone. Fushimi had laid out the exact things each of us had to focus on.

"Ugh."

"Let's start with a thirty-minute session."

She's for real...

I started putting my things on the same table when she said, "No, you can do it on your own desk. We'd focus better that way, too."

She's really for real...

Fushimi, however, always got mad when I tried to study at my own desk.

Torigoe detailed for me Fushimi's instructions, and I got going on the workbook as she did.

"".….."."

Was there any point in her coming to my house?

I glanced at her; she was solving exercises in the workbook, too.

The scritches of our mechanical pencils were the only sounds in the room.

"…Does Fushimi come here often?"

"Huh? Um, yeah, from time to time."

Scratch, scratch, scratch, crack.

"Oh…"

"What?"

"Is there any reason you're still not dating?"

"Huh?"

"Sorry, forget about it."

No, I wanted to know what she meant. *She asked why we're not dating, right? She means Fushimi, right?*

From an outsider's perspective, you'd think there'd be way more reasons to date her than to not.

Why we're not dating… Why we're not dating… Why we're not dating… Huh?

The biggest thing was that I still didn't know what *love* was. Probably hard to believe from a second-year high schooler, but it was the truth.

Thirty minutes had passed while I was busy navel-gazing, and Torigoe's timer started ringing.

"Ready for a break?"

I turned to look at Torigoe. "…Hey."

"What is it?"

"You said you loved me, right?"

"………Y-yeah……… Wh-why the question all of a sudden?"

She turned her head down.

Oh? She's getting red.

"What does that mean?"

"Huh?"

"It gets your heart rate up in manga and stuff, right?"

If there really was a convenient *thump-thump* sound effect in real life, then I'd know. Sadly, reality wasn't made that way, probably. I could tell because other effects, such as *fap-fap*, didn't actually sound in reality. I knew that from experience.

"...Please don't ask me that..."

"You think Shinohara could tell me?"

"I wonder what Mii even liked about you."

"Torigoe, you're just asking for karmic retribution."

"..."

It was weird. Torigoe didn't seem like the type to be very interested in romance, and yet, she was in love with me enough to ask me out.

"Is it some sort of undiscovered form of energy?"

What kind of fuel would make the usually quiet Torigoe do all that?

"What are you talking about?"

"Like, you know, the power of love."

"Please stop talking like an idiot who can't tell the difference between manga and reality."

"You're so witty today, aren't you, Torigoe?"

Torigoe leaned back, sitting in a more relaxed pose, and grabbed a manga from my box shelf.

"This title...and this one..."

"What about them?"

"These are the ones Fushimi has read, aren't they?"

"Yeah, I probably lent them to her. I haven't heard about her reading any others."

"..." Torigoe stared at the manga in silence. "If I... If I recommend you another novel, will you read it?"

She'd lent me a thin paperback a while ago, but I honestly didn't get it.

"A novel? Um… So long as the Bs don't, y'know, L, then yeah. Bring 'em."

Torigoe giggled. "Don't worry. I don't recommend them to people I don't think will like them."

"G-good to hear."

"I'll bring one next time. Read it."

"Sure."

I was interested in what title the big novel fan could possibly want me to read so much. Plus, she seemed happy about the prospect.

"I thought you'd be the kind to never read novels."

"I just read more manga."

She started asking me more about my tastes: what sort of genre I liked, if I preferred happy endings or sad endings, and such.

"…Lend me something you like, too."

"I only have manga for guys. That okay?"

I stood up and started scanning my collection. I gave her a quick summary of a few candidates as I pulled them from the crate.

"What's this one about?" Torigoe grabbed one that was just lying around.

"Ah, that's…"

Crap.

"…"

It was a porn manga I'd only changed the cover for.

"You… Y-you perv…" Torigoe closed it in a hurry and threw it at me.

"S-sorry… I'm…sorry…"

I thought she'd play it a bit cooler, but she lowered her red face.

…*Th-this is awkward. Oh boy.*

Fushimi would've screamed, which was easier to deal with, in a way.

"I—I already knew boys read things like that, but that was more… intense than I'd imagined." She'd gotten a real eyeful in only a few seconds. "Do you do that sort of thing with Fushimi?"

"What? O-of course not."

"I see… Even though you do kiss?"

"Huh?"

"Nothing," she said, grabbing her mechanical pencil again. "Anyway, choose a manga to lend me."

"Y-yeah…"

She saw?

It's not like there was anything bad about that. Not like I was even dating Torigoe. There was no need to make up any excuse. And yet… when she'd mumbled, *"Nothing,"* she did look hurt. I didn't know what to tell her.

This feeling inside me wasn't heavy enough to be guilt exactly, but it wasn't light enough to be just awkwardness, either.

"Ryou, did something happen with Torigoe?"

It was after school, just a few days before midterms. We were on our way home after studying, all three of us together.

"Something? Like what?"

"That's what I want to know."

What immediately came to mind was the expression she'd had on her face when she visited my house to study the other day. I didn't do anything wrong, but I still felt like I had. Perhaps I'd been subconsciously keeping my distance from her.

"Nothing happened," I told her.

I did feel bad for upsetting her so much, and for seeing it, too. It felt like something too private.

I hadn't read much of the novel she'd lent me, either, even though Fushimi said it was a *"good choice, very much like her,"* when I told her the title.

"...I could've lent you that one myself, too," she muttered, pouting.

The three of us went to hang out at a family restaurant after school, once midterms were finally over. Shinohara met up with us, too.

We were catching up on whatever when Fushimi said, "Let's have a postmortem for our tests and studying sessions." She crossed her arms above the table.

""" """
...

Are you serious? The question was painted on all three of our faces.

"Fushimi, we still haven't gotten our results back yet. Can't we do that then?"

"We should be ordering our food first, actually," Shinohara said, obviously annoyed, then started studying the menu.

"Ryou, how was your experience?"

"Well...normal for me?"

"Oh, that's not good news, Takaryou..."

Shinohara's school had also finished midterms already. She didn't seem to struggle enough to need to be joining us in our study sessions; in fact, I was guessing she had good grades.

"'Normal for you' isn't good enough, Ryou..."

"Hey, stop giving me that pitiful look."

We ordered our food, then talked about the contents of the tests, then about some random TV show, and on and on through various tangents and rabbit trails.

"Takaryou, want me to fill your drink?"

"Oh, I'll go myself. Thanks." I stood up, empty cup in hand.

"Girls sure talk about lots of things, huh..."

"Of course. That's what friends do."

Shinohara was grabbing some ice with tongs when I decided to ask her the question that had popped into my head the other day:

"Shinohara—you really didn't ask me out because of some dare, right?"

"Yes, I already told you. Why?"

"What did you like about me, then?"

"Huh?"

"I just...never asked, so I was wondering."

Not like I'd had many chances to do so during our three-day relationship.

"Well... I..."

She kept on putting ice into her cup.

It's already full, dude. Look out.

"I didn't save you from some delinquents; we didn't bump into each other at a corner. Was there any trigger for it?"

"…It's already over. Is there any reason for me to say that after so long?" She looked away, annoyed.

That's true.

I was just wondering if that'd help me as a reference point for what love was.

"Oh! It's Shino!"

I turned back and found Akiyama, from the class right next to mine. She was our classmate back in middle school. She was holding an empty cup, and I could see her two friends over at a table a ways from ours.

"It's been so long—how've you been?" "You've changed a lot," etc., etc. They didn't seem like friends back then, but from this conversation, it felt like they were at least pretty comfortable with each other.

"By the way, do you still do that?" Akiyama made a wry smile. "That thing—'the path of your fate' thing or whatever that was."

Her tone was pretty casual, but I could sense the scorn in it, too.

"Not anymore," Shinohara answered, her smile stiff.

"You went to Seiryo because you didn't want people knowing, didn't you?"

"…No."

"Huuuh? Reaaally?"

That might've been just a little banter had they been real friends, but Shinohara's behavior suggested that wasn't the case. Akiyama probably was sincere, though.

I interrupted her. "She's saying no, so let's leave it at that, okay?"

"But everyone says—"

"She went to Seiryo because she's smart. That's it. There's no funny reason behind it all—too bad."

Akiyama couldn't reply to that. The mood stayed awkward while we got our drinks, then left. On our way back, Shinohara said, "…That's why."

"Why what?"

"What you were saying."

"About you going to Seiryo?"

"N-no, I didn't go there to run away, and I wasn't trying to get a do-over or anything, okay? I just, um…"

"It's fine. Even if you did, even if it was because you wanted to leave your edgelord self behind, what's the matter? Who cares?"

"I *just* said it's not that!"

"Fine, fine. Don't get mad at me."

It was pretty suspicious how she always got heated when the topic came up, though.

"That…that was my 'saved from delinquents,' my 'bump at the corner' back then."

But I didn't do anything? Seriously, I don't get smart people.

14) I Don't Get "Love"—Part 2

"What exactly went on?"

"Gosh, you're so annoying…"

I was back home after our review session with Fushimi, interrogating Shinohara. I could easily picture her grumpy face on the other side of the phone, but I didn't stop.

"We were in the same group for the field trip in second year of middle school, right? Was it then?"

"I forget."

"C'mon. Tell me, please."

I was asking her about why she fell in love with me back then. She sighed in resignation and finally gave an answer.

"The trigger was…the field trip, I think. The others were all walking so fast, and I couldn't keep up, but you were the only one who waited for me…"

That happened?

"Wait, that's it?"

"Th-that was just the beginning! The trigger, I said! …You started getting my attention after that…"

"That was really enough to get your attention?"

"Who cares! Leave me alone! Also…you should be asking this to someone else… This is so embarrassing, God."

"I'm feeling awkward, too."

"You stupid…"

The only reason I could ask her directly was because I didn't even know who else to ask. Besides, solving the mystery behind why she'd asked me out would be completely worth it, I thought.

"Don't Fushimi or Shii grab your attention in any similar way? Not like friends but like…girls."

The thing that made me the most conscious of it was the kiss, but I wasn't going to tell her. That wasn't exactly fair anyway, since we hadn't followed the proper steps.

"Well, I won't say no…"

"By the way, which one? Fushimi or Shii?"

She sounds excited now. "Both, I guess. I have fun with both of them and feel at ease when we're together alone."

"Does your heartbeat speed up and stuff?"

Now that was probably a no for both.

"Do you feel happy just seeing their faces, or like you could get through anything that comes your way the rest of the day because you got to say hi?"

"Um, what?"

She sighed for what seemed like an eternity. *"Yeah, just die alone."*

"Hey, stop." *What did I do to deserve death?* "Do you think I'm weird?" I asked.

"Yeah. You'd be less weird if you were off going through your edgy teen phase. You haven't had your first love yet, Takaryou?" She sounded exasperated.

Is it really that weird to not understand love?

There were a few guys in class with girlfriends. They didn't tell me personally, but I'd heard the rumors. Still, I wasn't jealous at all. I won't deny I had a sex drive, and interest in sex as such, but that didn't mean I'd fall in love. That wasn't a conclusion you'd reach by seeing the other person naked in the first place, I thought.

"Was I your first love, Shinohara?"

"Too bad. I had it back in preschool."

Wow, that's early.

"I think girls start feeling these emotions earlier than boys, but you're a pretty late bloomer even by those standards."

"That's why I'm asking these things, you know?"

"Ughhh," she groaned. *"Look, a proper lady like me shouldn't be saying this, but... D-do you sometimes think of Fushimi wh-when you're... Y'know?"*

"What?"

What the hell's she saying all of a sudden?

"I'm asking 'cause it's the only way I can imagine a guy thinking about this."

You're telling me to ask my d*ck?

"I have never done that while thinking about a real person."

"S-so you do do it..."

"Well, yeah."

"Uh-huh..."

Then a moment of silence.

"Wait, are you imagining me doing it or something?"

"O-of course not! I—I was just thinking about how you're really just like any other boy..." She cleared her throat. *"W-well then, let's change the question. Which one would you rather see naked?"*

"You're really just asking me this, huh?"

"And you can give more than one answer."

"You have no shame."

One of them naked...?

"I'm just changing my approach, since you keep saying you don't get it. You should be thanking me. My face is beet red right now, just so you know..."

"You're right. Sorry for making you do this, and thanks."

"Don't try and change the subject."

How did she know?

Besides, I think we're already going offtrack with this conversation.

We went from me not understanding love to finding out which of them I loved.

"Shii looks like she might have curves in all the right places."

"…" *Torigoe?*

"Stop picturing it."

"You're the one putting images in my head…"

"So Takaryou likes girls with secretly big boobs. Note taken."

"Don't take notes."

What's scary was that I couldn't tell what she was actually doing on the other side of the phone.

…*Wait? Secretly big boobs?*

Fushimi was completely flat from the front. Her body drew an exquisite straight line from the side. Zero curves.

I'd also seen her naked many times before, when we were little. Obviously there'd be some changes now, but I wouldn't say I really wanted to see her naked again.

"Huh? Wait a minute…"

We'd played a bunch of times in an inflatable pool at my home's small garden. I remembered someone else being there… Oh, Mana?

"Just study up by reading some girls' manga. Love is a misunderstanding or a wrong impression most of the time anyway."

What a weird feeling to have her be so blunt that far into the conversation.

"I'll lend you some if you don't have any," she said, giving me a few recommendations. I agreed to borrow one of them.

"I don't think I'd have any trouble if reading manga was all I needed to do."

Though maybe I was wrong. I'd never read girls' manga, after all.

"Bubby…who're you talking with?" Mana peeked into my room.

"Ah, with Shinohara."

"Oh, the Boss?"

The Boss?

Well, I could kinda tell why she'd start calling her that.

Mom was right… Mana's boobs *were* big. Impressively developed for a middle schooler.

"Bubby's staring at my boobs…!"

"You can tell?"

"Of course. Wanna touch?"

"No."

I decided to ask Mana my question, too. "Mana, what is love for you?"

"For me?" She tilted her head and thought for a bit before answering. "It means caring more for that person than I do for myself, I think." She giggled timidly.

"Oh, I see."

"G-good night!" Mana ran away, perhaps out of embarrassment.

That answer was about ten times more useful than anything the Boss had said.

"How was it?" Torigoe asked me during lunch break in the physics room.

"How was what?"

"The novel I lent you."

Oh right, I haven't even opened it. "I haven't read it yet... Sorry."

"Oh. Tell me if it doesn't seem like you'll enjoy it. I'll lend you another one."

"Yeah, thanks." I glanced at her a few seats away.

"...What's wrong?"

"Oh, no, nothing."

"Shii looks like she might have curves in all the right places."

I couldn't get Shinohara's words out of my head.

Really...? Seriously? I wondered, glancing to find out. It really didn't seem like it, but maybe there was something I was missing from Shinohara's point of view as a fellow girl. The Boss had said *"secretly big boobs,"* so maybe it was something you couldn't just tell from a glance.

"Why are you looking at me so much? If you have anything to say, then just go ahead."

"No, it's nothing. Don't mind me."

"?" She frowned in suspicion.

She then started asking about the manga I'd lent her. I made sure not to spoil the story while I answered questions about which characters I liked, what I thought about them, and all that fun stuff.

"I wonder why all the female villains have huge boobs."

"Huh? Boo... Huh?"

"...Why so nervous? They do, don't they?"

For a moment there, I thought she noticed me looking again, but no. I sighed in relief.

This was all Shinohara's fault. She'd cursed me. She'd brainwashed me with the magic words *"secretly big boobs"* so I would stare at Torigoe's chest all the time.

"Uhhh, yeah, they do. It happens. Lots of sexy villains."

"They would be impressive on a figure. Yeah, that would be crazy." She nodded to herself. "Do you like them big, too, Takamori?"

"Huh? What are we talking about, again?"

"You know very well what. Boobs."

My gaze instinctively drifted to her chest. I shook my head to get rid of the worldly thoughts.

"I guess I'd say...big, if I had to choose?"

"I see."

Torigoe kept a poker face, but I could tell she was clenching her fist in celebration below the desk.

Do you realize I can see you do that?

"I see; I see. Hmmmm. So you like them big," she repeated, acting all cool and calm about it.

Since she keeps saying it over and over, then maybe...it's true? But it doesn't seem like that at all from her uniform. What is even going on with her chest?

"L-let's stop talking about this, okay?" This was getting really awkward, so I tried to change the subject. "Okay then, what about you? What's your big turn-on?"

"Voice."

That was fast!

She didn't look embarrassed in the slightest; in fact, it seemed like she had some pride in it.

"Like Yoshiyoshi's, the voice actor."

Who's that? Is that a fan nickname?

"Well, that's very specific."

So…does that mean my voice piqued her interest?

"You don't have that, though. I think turn-ons and what you love are different things."

"I guess that might apply to me, too, then."

"Oh, is that so?"

Her voice was lower now.

"Takamori, you've been staring at my chest this whole time, haven't you?"

"Huh? N-no…"

"Don't lie—I can tell."

Seriously? Come to think of it, Mana said the same thing. So it wasn't some gyaru *superpower, huh?*

"I don't really mind…"

You don't?

Her face started turning red. "But it is embarrassing, so I'd rather you stopped…"

"Sorry."

"This counts as sexual harassment, just so you know."

"I'm truly sorry."

"You boob maniac."

"Ugh, I have no defense…"

She giggled with a whisper. "I think that's the first time, so…"

So…?

I waited for the rest of the sentence, but she then grabbed her bag and stood up.

"Hey, don't leave me hanging."

"It's the first time you've looked at me that way, so…I—I'm kinda happy…but just a little," she muttered, then left the room, her face red as a tomato.

©Fly

"She's happy about that?"

About getting sexually harassed? Is she a pervert?

But she was right that I stared too much. Whoops. Maybe I was already conscious of her as a girl, as Shinohara had said. Maybe ever since that day she'd asked me out.

I went back to the classroom five minutes before class began.

"Fushimi, what's our next class?"

"I dunno."

…Huh? Is she mad at me or something?

Her bad mood went on even after school. I thought she'd leave without me while I was writing the class journal, but she stayed by my side. Though the mood was too awkward to chat in the meanwhile.

"You could just go home."

"That's not a nice thing to say to someone waiting for you, dude."

"Dude"?

"Did I do something? I apologize if so."

"You did something and you *didn't* do something."

"Is this a guessing game now? What did I do? Why are you mad?"

"You sexually harassed Torigoe."

And how do you know?

"She told me to be careful around you."

I got reported?! And to someone worse than the police!

"You never do that to me."

And that's why you're upset? Wait, that makes it sound like you want me to do it?

I mean…what can I even do? There's nothing to see there. Nothing to hide.

Looking at Torigoe's… Well, it had me feeling restless, but Fushimi's gave me more of a sense of security. I was already used to her figure, and I doubted it would ever change. Nice and stable. Or something.

"Boobs are no good, Ryou. They lead people astray," she said with absolute seriousness.

I could almost feel her eyes on me.

"F-fine, fine. I'll be more careful."

"...Ryou, I'm still developing, you know?"

"Let the record show that I said nothing." I chuckled while going back to writing the journal.

"My legs are pretty slender, if I do say so myself," she bragged. "Look." She stuck out her leg for emphasis.

"Stop it—you're almost showing your panties."

"Bwyah?!" She let out a bizarre scream, then held down her skirt. "You perv, perv, perv! Pig!"

"Stop acting like a kid." I sighed.

Fushimi laughed out loud. "...I don't mind showing you just a little..."

It was the first weekend after midterms. I had the perfect plans for the day: wake up just before noon, laze around watching TV, have a kind of brunch, then just play some games. But the world had something else in mind for me.

"Bubby? Hina's here!"

"Wha…?"

I woke up to Mana peeking in my room. I grabbed my phone. It was only eight in the morning. Three notifications were showing on the screen: all texts from Fushimi.

"What…?"

"I dunno—she's here to hang out, I guess?"

Why do these girls insist on coming at eight in the morning…?

"I can let her in, right? I mean, she's already right here behind me."

"She is…?"

My brain can't process anything right now. Please give me five minutes…

"Good morning, Ryou!" She popped up beside Mana. "Hee-hee. I caught you still asleep."

"Isn't Bubby so cute right after he wakes up?"

"Yeah, he is."

I got annoyed at them staring at me in the bed, so I rolled out from under the covers and sat on the floor.

"What are you doing here so early?"

"Um, well, I don't have anything special in mind." Fushimi giggled with a rueful smile.

"Oh, well. Torigoe's coming, too, anyway."

I guess it works out in the end.

"Ohhh… So *that's* why Hina came here so early," Mana commented.

"Shhh!" Fushimi hissed.

Mana nodded with a little sneer. "I get it; I get it. You were worried about the two of them getting together behind your back."

Yeah, Torigoe is her friend, too, so it makes sense Fushimi would want to join us. I agree that it doesn't feel quite right to now have two mutual friends hanging out together without me. Yeah, I get it.

"Bubby, I can tell by your face that you do not, in fact, get it."

"But I thought you'd be busy with school, Fushimi. I also didn't feel like I absolutely needed to tell you."

"That much is true, I guess."

"Hina, are you the possessive type?"

"C'mon, no!"

"I get it. Bubby might be dense and stupid as all hell, but that's what makes him endearing. You always feel more attached to the ones you need to take care of."

My little sister is giving me a motherly look…

"Have fun!" Mana said before pushing Fushimi into my room and slamming the door shut.

"I'll get changed."

"Ah! S-sorry. I won't look," she said, squeezing her eyes shut into a (>_<) emoji.

Then I got a text from Mana: She was going to bring breakfast, so she wanted me to tell her exactly when to enter. I answered while I was busy getting changed.

"You can open your eyes now," I told Fushimi.

I didn't mind her looking, but I supposed she did.

"Closing my eyes and hearing only the sounds you make is kinda... sexy..."

"You've seen me naked plenty of times before, right?"

"I mean, yeah..."

Shinohara's question about *"who'd you prefer seeing naked?"* then crossed my mind.

"But that was back when we were little. It's totally different now that we're in high school."

"..."

She still looks as flat as ever, though... Or has there been any change?

"What's wrong?"

"Ah, no, nothing."

Now I'm all sexually conscious. Damn you, Shinohara.

"So you don't have classes today?"

"They're in the evening. I'm free until then." She made a peace sign and beamed.

We talked about her acting for a bit while eating breakfast.

"They encouraged me to pick up some novels on top of watching dramas or movies. They say it helps with your expression."

So that's why she started reading.

She'd never struck me as a bookworm, so now it made sense why she was suddenly into it.

"Ryou, what do you usually have the most fun doing?"

"I guess playing games or reading manga..."

"You should start thinking about what you *want* to do."

"Yeah...," I said, but something didn't sit right with me.

Liking something didn't mean you'd do it as a job. Fushimi probably saw things differently—she was a go-getter, with a "main character" view of the world. Or was I just too passive, too apathetic? I felt like my perspective was the normal one.

Fushimi then talked about movies. She went on and on about director such-and-such and actress what's-her-name. I think everyone gets extra talkative about the things they love.

"I'm here," Torigoe called from outside before opening the door and peeking her head in.

It wasn't until then that I noticed I had a text from her saying, I'm here, and another one from Mana saying, I'll bring Tori upstairs, okay?

"I was wondering about that other voice I heard... Didn't expect you here, Fushimi."

"Good morning, Torigoe."

"...Yeah... Good morning."

"" ...""

It felt like time had stopped, and they were speaking through their eyes.

What's going on?

"Hey. Come in."

"'Kay." Torigoe entered the room, then sat on my bed, just like Fushimi.

They glanced at each other, then stayed quiet.

...Seriously, what's happening in here?

Torigoe did say she'd come by, but we didn't plan for anything in particular. Fushimi's appearance was more than unplanned for, though.

What I decided to do then to calm down the mood was recommend a boys' manga I'd been really into. They listened attentively to my passionate review, and they started reading Volume 1 together. Such good friends.

Meanwhile, I got to editing the video Mana had asked me to a while before.

"What are you doing, Ryou?"

"Is that a game?"

I didn't even look up from my phone. "Mana said she wanted to post a video of the fireworks from the other day, but she's bad with this kind of thing, so she gave me the clips to edit them into something better."

""Huh, is that so?""

Such good friends.

We commoners had to use phones instead of PCs. I could easily find dedicated apps that didn't need any technical knowledge or skill, though maybe what I was about to do was child's play from a professional editor's point of view. For me, this would take some time and effort, but I could manage a simple video.

"There we go."

I finished the barbecue fireworks video after about thirty minutes of trial and error.

"Lemme see, Ryou."

"I wanna see, too."

"Fine, but don't expect anything amazing."

""Just show me.""

They both peeked at my phone as I played the file I'd sent Mana.

She'd given me four clips. I cut out the best parts to make a twenty-second compilation. I'd put on some filters to make them look better and added a hip-hop track she liked. It was a pretty decent result, if I did say so myself.

"Ooooh. The fireworks look so pretty." Fushimi sighed. She sounded like a grade schooler.

Meanwhile, Torigoe's review: "In a short little clip, you showed not only the fireworks but also the people playing with them and how much fun they're having. It's pretty immersive."

Fushimi stared at her with shock, then cleared her throat. "Yeah. And the song is a good fit. This is a very trendy kind of video."

"Fushimi, it's not a competition."

She pouted; then they watched the video again.

"I didn't know you could do this, Ryou."

"It was all the app."

"But not everyone puts in the effort."

Torigoe nodded in agreement. "Editing work is boring and tiresome. I'd say most people just trim some parts before uploading."

"Yeah. Meanwhile, Mana's pretty serious about her posts. She gets so excited about all the likes that it makes me want to do the best I can, too."

I actually looked forward to her reports. My own account, on the other hand, was languishing in obscurity.

"I think you're the type to get more fun out of seeing other people having fun." Fushimi smiled.

We were eating curry for lunch when Fushimi asked, "Don't you think it'd be easier to edit if the clips were a bit different? Or that the video could've looked better?"

"Yeah, I do."

We were in my dining room, eating the food Mana had made in the morning. She had left for karaoke with her friends.

"That's why I edit them in the first place, to make the video look better."

"Right?! That's the thing, Ryou. Don't you think it'd be even better if you did it all yourself from the beginning?"

Sure, yeah.

"..." Torigoe listened to us in silence.

I was guessing Mana's curry was so delicious, it had rendered her speechless.

"S-so...wouldn't you like taking a video of me?"

"Of you?"

"J-just for practice. It might be a bit embarrassing getting recorded on video...but if it's for you, I don't mind it..." Her timid voice dropped to a mumble.

Fushimi was an actress-in-training. This would certainly serve her as practice.

"Yeah, sure."

"Huh? Really?"

"Mm-hmm."

Fortunately, I had upgraded my phone that spring to a top-of-the-line model. It had a pretty decent camera.

"This'll be good practice for both of us," she commented.

"How is it practice for me?"

"Well…if you want to work as a video editor?"

"Why would I?" I laughed.

"Because you seemed to be having fun with it."

"You think?"

"Yeah." She nodded.

"I agree," Torigoe added. "I didn't expect it, honestly. I thought you'd hate this. Isn't it too much trouble for you?"

Maybe I wasn't aware of it myself?

Setting aside how much fun I actually might have had, it was true that I didn't hate it or see it as tiresome.

"Do we try taking a video right now?"

I'd finished eating before the two of them, so I opened my camera app and switched it to video mode. I got Fushimi in frame. She was about two-thirds through her curry.

"Huh? Right now?"

"Right now."

"Whaaa…? B-but what do I do? I'm not prepared." She grabbed her cup with both hands in a panic and pretended to take a sip.

"I guess we need a plan, huh…," I commented. *Even though you were the one who suggested it…*

"How about we make a common account and upload our videos there?" Torigoe said.

""Ohhh...""

"Huh? What?"

It was easier to come up with ideas for video once you had an objective.

"Yeah, let's try that."

"When did Ryou become so assertive?"

"He's really into the idea, huh."

They looked at each other, then giggled.

We went back to my room after lunch.

I pointed the camera at Fushimi, who was sitting on my bed, and said, "Okay, let's start with a self-introduction."

"Okay. Yup, that's pretty important." She cleared her throat. "Don't use any footage before this, okay?"

Fushimi's expression turned serious. "My name is Hina Fushimi. I'm sixteen years old and a student at a prefectural high school. I live with my dad and my grandparents."

Now what? she asked with a glance.

While I was thinking about what to say next, Torigoe wrote on her notebook. **Hobbies?**

Ah, yeah, that's pretty normal for a self-introduction.

"I like watching movies and reading books. I also enjoy acting, and I'm currently training to become an actress." She smiled timidly at the camera.

Oh, that smile will give all the boys watching this a heart attack; I can see it now.

Do you have a boyfriend? What kind of boys do you like? Torigoe once again asked in writing.

"I'm single. I like the kind of person who's...serious and makes me feel safe."

Hold up. This is starting to feel like the intro to a porno.

Have you had your first kiss?

"Huhhh? Do I have to say that?"

Torigoe nodded intensely, her face completely serious.

Fushimi was hesitant but then immediately pulled herself together once she remembered she was in front of the camera.

"Yes. Just once," she proudly confessed.

Torigoe turned to look at me with impressive speed and pressure. "Uh-huh…," she muttered.

What? What do you mean to say?

What about sex?

Torigoe. You're doing this on purpose, aren't you?

Fushimi's face instantly flushed bright red; then she answered in a panic. "N-no. I haven't."

Now she's really starting to look like a different kind of actress…

"So you don't have any experience, either?"

Either? Oh, is that a confession, Torigoe? I could hear you, y'know?

She seemed intent on further escalating things, so I grabbed her hand.

"Torigoe, quit it."

I stopped recording. She'd written down, Where are you most sensitive?

What are you trying to do with that information?

"Do you even actually want to know that?"

"No, but this is how these things go, right?"

And how do you know?

"What is it?" Fushimi asked with the brightest, purest smile.

"Nothing… Torigoe, why do you even know 'how these things go'?"

"…" She looked away. She could dish it out, but she couldn't take it, huh.

"Ah, I should get going. I won't make it if I stay here any longer."

"Want me to take you to the station?"

I felt Torigoe glaring at me.

"Thanks, but I'll go to my house, and Dad will take me from there. Don't worry."

Fushimi grabbed her stuff, said good-bye, and left the room.

I played the video we'd just recorded. The fact that she was sitting on a bed the whole time just made it look even more wrong. In fact, it was hard to see it as anything *but* wrong.

"Takamori, it's your fault for having her sit on the bed for a self-introduction."

"We could've made this perfectly wholesome if it weren't for your questions. You're so bad, honestly..." I sighed.

Torigoe kept smiling; she probably didn't think of it as more than a little joke.

But really, how does she know how those sorts of videos go?

"I have some interest in it myself, you know?"

"Huh? In what?"

"Like, obviously I don't know anything about it. I haven't done it myself. I wouldn't want to get panicked if it did happen eventually, so I need to at least have some previous knowledge... So that's why..." Torigoe's face started turning progressively redder and redder. "Anyway, forget it! Forget this all happened!"

"Okay. I'll pretend I didn't hear that." I moved my hands up and down, trying to soothe her.

"Yes. I'd be glad if you did... And stop looking at me," she said, her hands covering her face.

"By the way, by 'taking her to the station,' did you mean you'd take her on your bike or something like that?"

"Hmmmm... I'll leave that up to your imagination."

"Meanie. You're awfully evil for a class president."

"I'm not the prez. Just a class rep."

Torigoe then moved behind me. *Does she not want me seeing her that badly?*

"She'd hug you from behind, right?"

"Maybe not hug, but I guess she'd put her arms around my waist."

"I see... Not fair."

Then Torigoe did just that. She was way too close—and I could feel her against my back.

"L-like this?"

"Y-yeah... Like that..."

Her chest was the only thing that felt different from Fushimi.

"Your back is pretty good."

"I think it's pretty average."

How long are you going to do that for?

It wouldn't feel right to tell her to let me go, and besides, there was nothing for us to do once she was done. I didn't know what to do.

She put her head on my back, then stayed that way for a while. Finally, she released me and all of a sudden said, "I'm going home," and rushed out.

"It's time for our first meeting in preparation for the school festival!" Waka said as soon as our long homeroom period started.

"Oh, it's already that time of the year!" Fushimi said, not a shred of worry in her voice.

I wasn't as optimistic, though; these kinds of meetings usually dragged, since it was so hard to reach an agreement. The end of May could seem early for the festival, but it was easier to get things going by starting right around that time...or so they say. In any case, we'd also started around that time last year.

"All right, class reps, the floor is yours." Waka grabbed the attendance book and left the classroom.

I resigned myself and followed Fushimi up to the front of the class.

"Does anyone have any ideas?" she asked.

Everyone looked to the side and talked with their neighbors, but nobody gave any suggestions. I'd taken the secretary role, chalk in hand, but it was ending up without use like this.

I mean, yeah, it's not The First or The Last school festival, so I can see why nobody's too eager. Not that I'd be into it then, either.

We were also missing a class clown, so we had nobody to be like, *This is our first and last school festival as second-years! Let's do it, guys!*

"How will we decide this?" Fushimi turned to me and asked, concern on her face.

"Well, we won't decide anything if no one throws out an idea or two... I doubt there's anything anyone wants to do in the first place."

I sure didn't care. The problem wasn't that people weren't willing to suggest something; it was that there was nothing to suggest.

"Whaaa—? Really?" Fushimi frowned, then groaned.

I looked at the class, and although there were some groups chatting, no one seemed to be intent on saying anything out loud.

"Well, we have Hina. How about we do a café, and we have her as our poster girl?" one of the girls said.

Café. Got it.

I wrote the idea down on the chalkboard. **Café + poster girl**, I was sure to add.

No idea who suggested it, but we couldn't judge it when there were no others to compare.

"Why build it around me?"

"That's just how it is."

"Then let's involve all the girls! I don't want to stay in the classroom all the time because of that."

Good point.

"Okay then, a maid café," a boy suggested.

A bit cliché maybe, but we already had one café idea, so it was fine by me.

"The boys just want us to wear sexy outfits!"

"Maids are not sexy!"

Finally, some discussion. Go ahead, but please don't focus on whether maids are or aren't sexy.

"A maid café, huh... What do you think, Ryou?"

I tried picturing Fushimi in a maid outfit. "Oh... Not bad."

"I see."

The ice was now broken, and ideas started pouring in one after the other, sometimes receiving opposition from the boys, sometimes from the girls. There was always someone against any given idea. We reached six suggestions total.

"How about we hold a vote?" Fushimi asked, troubled.

I shook my head. "We'd be forcing the people who are against them. We still have time, so how about we only leave it at the brainstorming step for today?"

"Yeah, you're right." She stared at me.

"What is it?"

"Nothing. I was just thinking about how reliable you are sometimes."

Cool. "You don't have any ideas yourself?"

"Well, I kinda do, but I don't."

And what does that mean?

I turned to look at Torigoe, but she shook her head.

Not even you, huh.

On the teacher's desk was a paper with the rules regarding exhibits and performances for the school festival. We could either do exhibits or shops in the classroom or performances on the school gym's stage. We couldn't just make the classroom a free resting space the way we did last year. Performances at the gym had to fit within a schedule, first come, first served.

"How about a solo play by you, Fushimi?"

"No, I don't think so…"

"It was a joke."

And yet, she was kinda taking it seriously.

"We can't just leave all the work to you. This is supposed to be a collaborative effort."

"Y-yeah. It's better for everybody to work together. Young and old."

"Yes. We're all the same age, though."

A class was always a hodgepodge of personalities; this was an important opportunity for introverts and extroverts to come together.

However, just as I expected, discussion petered out after the relatively strong start, and no more ideas were given.

That's how I'd expect this to go at the beginning, yeah.

Waka probably saw that coming, which was why she'd said it was our *first* meeting.

"We aren't in agreement on any of these ideas, huh?"

"Yeah. I think everyone knows clearly what they *don't* want to do, at least."

And saying *everything's fine by me* can also actually mean *nothing's fine.* No two people have exactly the same preferences, and getting thirty people to agree on one thing was no easy feat.

"Okay then, how about we first say what we don't want to do?" That way, they wouldn't be able to oppose so easily after the fact.

Luckily, I said that right when everyone else was quiet, so they all heard me.

"Nice idea, Prez!"

"Yeah, it might be easier to come up with what we don't want to do first."

"Good one, Prez!"

"I'm telling you, I'm not the prez. Class rep."

How many times must I repeat myself?

Torigoe, too, was nodding to herself, her face as inexpressive as usual.

"Sounds good," said Fushimi, and then it was settled.

Everyone started stating what they didn't want to do.

"No maids or cosplay," the girls said.

Yeah, that's too much.

Fushimi and Torigoe agreed, too.

"I don't want anything that doesn't involve the girls doing cosplay," one of the boys said.

Come on, dude.

Of course, the girls immediately went after him.

"We don't want the boys giving us sick, horny looks because of those stupid sexy maid costumes."

"Maids are not sexy!"

Why are you so passionate about that point?

I sighed and wrote down what they said.

"I… I'm okay with whatever everyone agrees on. I can trust Fushimi and Prez to do the right thing. I won't complain about anything that comes up," one of the boys said.

Hey, I think we could be friends… I'll try speaking to him sometime… It might already be the end of May, but maybe I can still do it.

Then came Torigoe's turn.

"…I do *not* want to do a play that could lead to a couple falling in love. No *Romeo and Juliet* or anything like that."

She really stressed the *"do* not *want"* part.

Also, that's quite specific…almost like she's addressing one particular person…

Fushimi quietly opposed it. Her cute face was twisted in discontent and possibly disbelief.

And we've found the expression! That face is really counteracting all your charm.

"Now, President Ryou, what about you? What's your take on the worst school festival?"

"What, is this hot-take expo now?"

It feels close, but that wasn't the idea, y'know?

"I'd like an idea where everyone can work on something individually. Something that won't have people pushing the work onto others."

"Ryou… Bravo!"

Please don't clap.

"Well said, Prez!"

"That's why you're the prez!"

"Yeah, it doesn't feel right when some people get to do nothing."

They all agreed with me. People soon started shifting from *I don't want this* to *How about we do this?*

"Yes, yes. Very good." Fushimi, quite pleased, scanned over the ideas on the blackboard.

The last bell of the day finally rang, signaling the end of class.

I copied the ideas from the blackboard to my notebook while Fushimi wrote in the journal.

"I think most of the plays aren't allowed, though," she said.

"Something wrong?" Torigoe sat down on the seat in front of mine.

"Not really, but your requirement basically ends up banning all stage plays, so we have a narrower selection."

"Some plays don't have a couple as protagonists, right?"

"Ugh…"

Torigoe had the upper hand in verbal warfare.

"But if these are the only things they opposed, then I can be sure my idea will get passed," Fushimi said with a sudden smirk on her face.

What are you plotting?

"I'll stop your schemes," Torigoe replied, ready to take her head-on.

I really had no idea if they actually got along or not.

"Study this." Shinohara gave me a bag of girls' manga and immediately left.

It wasn't that I *wanted* to read them; they'd serve as reference, at least. But...

"This is too much..."

How many volumes are there here?

"Bubby, is someone visiting?"

"Shinohara just came to lend me some girls' manga, but she already left."

"Uh-huh."

I was actually pretty grateful she'd come all this way on a weeknight.

"What kind of relationship do you have with the Boss?"

"Well..."

I didn't want to tell her she was my ex...after a three-day relationship.

"We were classmates back in second year of middle school. She's also an old friend of Torigoe's, so."

"Hmm."

I carried the heavy paper bag up the stairs while Mana followed.

"What?" I asked.

"I wanna see what they are."

"Okay." I gave it no further thought and entered my room.

The manga was neatly ordered by series, so it was easy choosing one. There were four series, a total of forty-six volumes. No wonder it was heavy.

I sat on my bed; then Mana did so, too, beside me.

"Oh, they're all already finished," she said as soon as she saw the titles.

I didn't think she'd know anything too obscure, so I guessed they were all major titles.

"Then let's just start with this one." I grabbed a book at random; then Mana peeked in from the side. "Isn't it hard to read like that?"

"Don't worry. Go on. I'm curious, too."

Mana stuck close to me while she perused the book in my hands. I told her I'd lend it to her later, but she just told me to flip to the next page already. I decided not to argue and continued reading.

"...So in this one, the plain girl comes across the hottest guy in class, huh. Classic setup."

"Is that so?"

"Yup. Hee-hee-hee. It's just like you."

"How?"

"Just flip the boy's and the girl's positions."

You mean Fushimi and me? But we've always been close, so it's a bit different from this.

It took me a while to get used to it. Maybe since I never read girls' manga.

"Oof... My heart..." Mana reacted to the saccharine developments.

You having a heart attack or something?

"Mana, you said that *love* means caring more about the other person than yourself, remember?"

"Mmm? So?"

"Don't you think that's impossible unless it's someone you already know to some extent?"

In this manga, the protagonist was already in love with the hero before the end of Volume 1. It hadn't even been a month.

Is it the face? Is that really it? Can handsomeness win out over time together?

"Hmm, maybe. I mean, the only one I really love for now is you, so that's the only point of reference I've got." She pouted.

So I guess I've got no 'point of reference' so far, to use her expression?

"Does that mean you still haven't had your first love?"

"Hee-hee-hee. You're my first love, Bubby. ♡"

She grabbed me by the arm.

You cute, silly little girl.

She had absolutely no relationship with any guys; she really was nothing like the *gyaru* stereotype.

"Why do you ask all this? Do you want to fall in love with someone, Bubby?"

Want to fall in love with someone… I never even considered it like that.

I didn't know how to answer, so I flipped the page to stall for time.

"Is it Hina? Or Tori?"

"I don't know."

It wasn't about choosing either or—I didn't even know how I'd choose.

"Then—then what about me? Do you love me? Or do you hate me?"

"If I have to choose, then love."

"Nice."

She made good food, took care of me, and heard me out when I needed to have a serious talk.

"Then what about Hina? Tori? The Boss? …You wouldn't hang out with them if you hated them, right? You're not the type to do that. So that means you love them all, to a certain extent."

"I guess."

"But, well, it's probably more *like* than *love*. However, I doubt it's the same for each one of them. Surely there's a difference in the shape or quality those feelings take for you. Um…how do I put this?" She thought hard. "You just focus on how you want to care about them—that's it. It's fine if you don't *love* love them."

How I want to care about them, huh… I never thought of it like that.

"Who's your number one of that list?" Mana asked, her eyes shining bright.

"I still don't know. That's the problem, y'know?"

"Geez! This is where you're supposed to say, 'It's you, Mana,' in your most handsome voice. Read the mood! And don't forget to grab me by the chin and stare right into my eyes while saying it!"

"You're too hard to please."

"Maybe you can't even tell your own feelings, huh, Bubby?" Then she patted my head for some reason. "I don't think anyone in real life actually falls in love just like in manga. No one follows the procedures."

Now she'd completely refuted Shinohara's whole point about me studying.

"You see how unusual things happen in real life, such as little sisters falling in love with their big brothers, right?"

"Huh?"

"Hee-hee. Though I guess that happens in manga, too."

...You were also just talking about it a second ago, weren't you?

That she had no other point of reference. That the point was thinking about how you want to care about them. Perhaps Mana's feelings didn't fit the common standards of romance, but maybe for her, that was still love, and that was good enough.

"That's pretty deep for a *gyaru*."

"I am smarter than you, after all. And being a *gyaru* has nothing to do with it." She giggled timidly.

I kept reading while she was still clinging to me, until she stood up a few minutes later.

"Gee, I can't keep reading this with you here!" She covered her relaxed face with both hands and left the room; then from outside, she said, "I'll borrow it later to read it by myself!"

"Okay."

There were many scenes of the protagonist getting flustered after her interactions with the hero, and they were making her grin too hard.

The protagonist must have seen all those *thump*, *ba-dump*, *eek*, and *squeal* sound effects and recognized her *love*, labeling it *romance*.

Maybe I was just dense to my own feelings, as Mana said. After all, I had felt those sound effects inside myself many times before.

Morning homeroom ended. When Waka left the classroom, Fushimi suddenly remembered and said, "Ah, today's the last day for everyone to turn in their career survey, so everyone who hasn't done so already, please give yours to us!"

Oh right, that was today.

The teacher probably forgot, too, since she didn't say anything. Impressive that Fushimi did remember. The classroom immediately turned noisy.

"Here you go, Prez." Honma, from the tennis club, left her survey on my desk. "Don't look."

"I didn't want to until you said that."

"Not like I wrote anything embarrassing, so I don't care." She grinned, turned around, and joined her group of friends.

So that means I can look, right?

All the boys, plus about half the girls, turned theirs in to Fushimi, so I had no idea what other people had written.

"..."

I flipped the paper on my desk to take a peek.

Cosmetology school, it said in cute, girly handwriting.

So Honma wants to be a beautician, huh.

Her second and third options were blank.

"Ryou, what about yours?" Fushimi asked while straightening her pile of papers.

I had shoved my survey into a corner without writing anything. I didn't come up with any brilliant ideas, so I hadn't even thought to take it out. Now it was all crumpled up.

"I can't imagine my future at all."

"Just write down what comes up for now. You don't have to think so hard about it." She giggled.

Said the person who thinks too hard about everything. Well, if she's saying it, I actually do feel a little better.

Torigoe brought me her survey. "Here."

"Yeah."

She went right back to her seat, and I glanced over what she'd written.

Public university. Faculty of literature. Preferably within the prefecture.

She did say she wanted to do humanities at a public college, but I didn't know she wanted literature.

"…"

And that was when I realized, after all this time, that universities had various faculties. You couldn't just do "humanities"—you also had to choose what branch you wanted to study.

"…Not like I'm going to study sciences anyway."

"Ryou!" She leaned over to me.

"Geez, that startled me. Wh-what is it?"

"I was just wondering—how long are you planning on calling me Fushimi?"

"How long…? Well, until you stop being Fushimi, I guess?"

"Listen to what I mean!"

"Whoa, calm down. What's wrong? Why are you shouting? Everyone's looking at us, see?"

She cleared her throat once she realized she had everyone's attention on her, then lowered her voice.

"You used to call me Hina back in grade school, and then you suddenly changed that in middle school. I didn't like it when you started calling me by my last name, you know?"

"…I was just embarrassed to call a girl by her first name."

"So that's why you're all, like, 'Fushimiii' now, you coward?"

Was that supposed to be an imitation of my voice? And why the insult?

"I'm not a coward."

It always catches me off guard when she gets all huffy like this.

"Ryou, listen. Fushimi is a place name."

"It's also your last name."

"Stop making excuses!"

"Oh right, you said you had a suggestion for our exhibition for the school festival, right?"

"Oh, yes. Hee-hee, it's very, very… Hey, don't try to change the subject!"

Damn, she noticed.

"You can just call me Hina, you know? It's fine. Don't feel embarrassed."

"I don't think that's how it works."

"Then give me a nickname. Like how Shinohara calls you Takaryou."

"Fushihina… That's too hard to say."

Come to think of it, I'd never come up with a nickname for her. I'd always just called her by her first or last name.

"How about Hiina?" Now she was making suggestions.

"Wait, are you jealous of people who call each other by nicknames?"

"Agh!"

"Can't believe you actually yelled in pain because I was right."

"It's all your fault… You always say my name like it's just some word…"

There are two kinds of people in the world: those easily nicknamed and those not easily nicknamed. Fushimi was quite obviously the latter. I couldn't exactly say why that was, but let the record state that giving her a nickname was not easy.

"Princess, then."

"I don't like that. It feels like you're putting me on a pedestal. If anything, it sounds like an insult."

I thought it fit her perfectly, however. The word, *hime*, even kinda sounded like her name.

After much trouble, I decided to summon Torigoe for help.

"Torigoeee? Fushimi says she wants a nickname."

"I don't think nicknames usually stick when you force it," she said, coming up to our seats.

"Mana's good at this stuff and still just uses Hina, so I don't think there's anything we can do."

"So she is good at it," Torigoe whispered, convinced. "She just sent me a text telling me Tori was hard to say, so she'd call me Shizu instead."

...*Shizu? Oh, because she's Shizuka?*

I glanced at her. Yeah, *Shizu* fit her perfectly. That nickname would be good even if it wasn't part of her name.

"Yeah, she's good."

"And if she's used to calling Fushimi by her name, then there's no need to change it, is there?" she said.

"Someone...please... Call me Hiina... I've been waiting for this ever since middle school..." Fushimi fell in a puddle on her desk.

Torigoe laughed and mercilessly cut down her hopes. "That sounds like the name of an underground idol." But then she added, "Fine, I'll call you that if you want."

"Torigoe!!" She stood up suddenly and energetically grabbed her hands.

"Hiina."

"Yes!"

Torigoe nodded. I could tell she was happy, too.

"So, Ryou, what will you do?" Fushimi asked, sitting right in front of me in the physics room, during a rare lunch break visit.

"Just out of curiosity, what did you write?"

"I..." She searched for her paper in her bag.

Actress

Actress

Actress

She'd written the same thing for all three options. Once again, I had trouble responding. It was so impressive that she had a goal to strive for and could proudly say it out loud.

"Takamori, what did you write?" Torigoe sat next to me. Another weird occurrence, since she always kept her distance when it was just the two of us.

"Still blank."

"Oh."

"Don't forget, today's the deadline! Waka will chew you out if you don't submit it!"

"I know; I know." I waved her off. "You're so lucky to have your sights set on something that clear."

"...You think so?"

There was something strange about the silence before her reply; her smile also seemed forced.

"Don't try to rush him, Hiina. We all go at our own pace."

"I'm not rushing anything. They decided the deadline a while ago, and it applies equally to all of us."

"Why did you come here today? What about your followers?"

"I brushed them off; don't worry."

You "brushed them off"? I just hope they don't come here looking for you again.

"What about you, Torigoe? You're always in a seat way over there—what's up today?"

"Nothing. I just thought it'd be strange to be far away by myself."

Am I just imagining things, or is the air around us getting heavier and hotter each time they open their mouths?

"W-well, let's set that aside for now and have lunch."

They both sighed at the same time.

Now what? What did I do?

We started eating, and during a lull in the conversation, Torigoe set her phone on the desk so that we could all see.

"I tried making the Fushimi account and posted that thing we did the other day."

"Hold on—you mean that interview on the bed?"

"Yes."

"Oh, really?" Fushimi said, completely optimistic.

She's so blissfully ignorant...

Torigoe had asked me to edit the video, and I'd given it a try, but I didn't think she'd actually post it online.

"It's getting tons of likes." She scrolled down to show the number of likes and comments.

"Three hundred?! And it's already past two hundred followers!"

"Huh? Wh-what? Is that a lot?" Fushimi looked at us with wide, innocent eyes.

"It's pretty impressive for a new account, yeah."

Most of the comments were from men. Thank God I'd edited out the part where she said her full name.

Oh, there it is. A comment asking if this is for a porno.

"You cut out the entire part where I say my name, though?"

"That's for the best."

It is? she asked me with a glance.

I nodded. "It's better to not let people know who you are in this kind of thing. You wouldn't want strangers going to your home after finding out you're Hina Fushimi, would you?"

"Eek…" Her face turned pale at the thought. "Do people have that much time on their hands?"

"Hiina, you sure you're from the twenty-first century?"

"I knew she was ignorant about the Internet, but I didn't realize it was this bad."

"Huhhh? Am I supposed to know more?"

Torigoe and I nodded at the same time.

"You're a granny both in cooking and Internet knowledge." Torigoe was not pulling her punches.

"Fushimi, remember when we were in middle school?"

"What? What happened then?"

She really doesn't know, huh.

Fushimi had a stalker back then, and she didn't even realize. Fortunately, it all got resolved without incident, thanks to some real scary glares from the older kids who liked her.

"Hiina, you should always remember that the Internet is a jungle."

"I see."

Her inability to sense danger was quite worrying.

"Well, now that that video's doing well, how about we take a second one?" Torigoe suggested.

"Fine by me!" Fushimi agreed; then they both looked at me, waiting for an answer.

"Sure, okay, let's do it." Not like there was any reason for me to object.

We spent the rest of lunchtime talking about what to do for the next video.

"Let's try getting more into specifics of what we talked about in the first video…"

Producer Torigoe started giving ideas. Neither Fushimi nor I had any special requests, so we immediately agreed.

"This is fun. I wonder if it'll feel the same way."

"What's 'it'?"

"The school fest—" Fushimi opened her eyes wide in realization, then stopped herself.

"Hiina, is there something you want to do for the school festival?"

"Something that doesn't violate any of the conditions we set, where all sorts of people can do their part…" I summarized the agreement we'd reached in our meeting.

"Maybe something like an independent film?" Torigoe said.

"Agh!"

"So that is what you're thinking."

An independent film…, I repeated to myself.

"Yeah, that was it. I was just thinking—might be fun to make one." Then she started timidly poking her food. "Ryou can direct, and Torigoe can write. What do you think?"

What do I think?

Torigoe seemed to feel the same; we turned toward each other at the same time.

"Of course, I'll play the main part," she said, and I could feel her strong ambition and will through her eyes and voice.

If any other girl said that, people might ask, *"Is she really the best for it, though?"* or, *"Shouldn't we first see if anyone else wants to do it, too?"* But no one would object to Fushimi. That was just how astoundingly pretty she was.

Some third-years back in middle school had held it against her for no reason, but that only hurt their own social status. Her popularity was as extraordinary as her looks.

Even just hearing her say, *"Of course, I'll play the main part"* felt like all was right in the world. She knew that was her territory, and that she wouldn't—couldn't—leave it up to someone else.

I had never seen her so firmly stand her ground. I was sure everyone would agree if she proposed it in our next class meeting.

"Her protagonist power is off the charts…"

Torigoe opened her mouth after a while. "Is that your first idea, Hiina? It feels like there's more." That was her way of politely opposing it.

"You think so?" Fushimi's face fell. "I'm sure you can do it. Both of you."

"Don't try to get people…Takamori involved in everything you want."

"That wasn't my intention…" Now Torigoe was starting to feel bad. "I'm sorry…" She closed her still-unfinished lunch box, grabbed her bag, and left the physics room.

"H-hey, Torigo—"

I peeked into the hallway just in time to see her wipe out.

Oh, man…

Her lunch spilled all over the floor. I sighed and approached her while scratching my head, then crouched down beside her.

"Are you okay? Anything hurt?"

"…Thanks. No, I'm fine. I'm sure you just think I'm sick in the head or something."

"I don't. Only surprised by how aggressive you can get against her."

"I just want one thing to go my way from time to time, you know?"

"Fushimi's on another level."

"She is."

I took a look at Torigoe and finally realized.

*   *   *

Fushimi had this passion for acting; she had dreams and the power of a protagonist to make it all happen. I felt inferior beside her. I had nothing. Even if I tried, I would never reach Fushimi's level of proficiency. Fushimi's presence made the people around her feel inferior. Just seeing her was enough to make you feel how tiny you were in comparison.

Of course, none of this was her doing, but just her presence was enough…

Then I heard Torigoe sniffle, and I saw her tears. I rubbed her back in silence.

"I…I want to know more about you, too. I want to fall even more in love with you, but that time will never come…"

Torigoe's cries, her unusually emotional voice, hit like a punch in the chest. But I didn't know how to react to what she'd said.

"Are you okay?!" Fushimi came out of the room. She was holding a broom and dustpan.

"Sorry. I was too aggressive."

"No, don't worry about it. C'mon—lunchtime is almost over. Let's pick this up."

We cleaned the hallway, then put away the broom and dustpan.

Perhaps Torigoe's objections and aggressiveness were simply her way of trying to get what she wished for.

After school, I was writing in the journal.

"Torigoe," Fushimi called.

"Oh, sorry, I have library duty today." With that, Torigoe left the classroom.

Fushimi came back to her seat with low energy. She dropped her shoulders like a beat-up boxer on break.

"Ryou, what should I do? …Torigoe hates me now…" She was about to cry, her eyes already welling up.

"She just said she had to go to the library, right? I don't think she hates you."

She was acting quite politely, all things considered. Fushimi was her friend but also her love rival, and she hadn't committed fully to either role.

"You think so…?"

I decided to get Shinohara to talk it out with Torigoe and check how she was actually feeling.

"Maybe she just didn't like your idea."

"You think so…?" Her voice got lower and lower, her face buried between her legs on the chair.

"Nothing wrong with an argument. Don't you know how they say only true friends get in arguments?"

"We're always glaring at each other, though."

"Huh?"

You are?

Meanwhile, I had no one to argue with. Maybe Shinohara was the closest it got? I was able to open up to her without any worry.

That was when Fushimi started crying for real. There was nothing I could do to get through to her, so I simply went on writing down in the journal what we'd learned in class that day.

Come to think of it, there was a scene like this in one of the manga I'd borrowed from Shinohara. A pair of close friends gets in an argument, and things become awkward between them afterward. In that story, the reason was because of a slight misunderstanding, but that wasn't really the case here. I didn't even feel like it was an argument, actually.

"Wanna go to the library after we get this to Waka?"

"I don't know… What if she ignores me?"

It was rare hearing her say something negative.

"We'll cross that bridge once we're there."

"You can't be that thoughtless!"

"How about we try practicing for it in case she does ignore you?"

"That sounds so sad..."

Finally, she agreed to go to the library.

We grabbed our bags and the class journal and headed for the staff room. Waka wasn't there, fortunately, so we just left the career survey submissions on her desk. I still hadn't filled mine out. She didn't even seem to remember the deadline, though, so I figured there would be no problem submitting it later that week.

We left the staff room and walked toward the library; on our way there, I could tell Fushimi was anxious.

"I'm sweating cold..."

"You see, she might be feeling anxious right now, too, thinking about a way to mend things."

"I hope so..."

She closed her eyes tight, then took several deep breaths.

"..."

She never showed that side of herself in the classroom; it was pretty cute.

I patted her hair, and she turned to look at me.

"Oh, sorry for touching you. Should've asked."

"No, don't worry. I was just surprised." Her face finally relaxed into a smile.

I put my hand back in my pocket, and she stared at it almost like she missed it.

"It'll all be fine."

I opened the door and entered. Torigoe was right there in the corner, reading a book. She seemed very focused—she didn't realize we were there.

There was no one else inside, perhaps because midterms had just ended recently.

"You don't seem to have much work."

"…Oh, Takamori."

"Fushimi's here, too." I pointed at my back.

"Huh? Hiina?"

Don't act like you can't see her, I thought while turning back, but no one was there. *Where did she go? She was here just now.*

"…"

Then she slooowly peeked her head around the still-open door.

"What're you doing there? Come in."

Fushimi darted in, then immediately hid behind me.

Why so shy?

"What's wrong?"

"Well, it's just…Fushimi was actually crying before in the classroom, because she thinks you hate her now."

Torigoe giggled. "Why?"

"I mean… You were so cold…," Fushimi hedged.

"That's just how she is—you didn't know?" I said.

"Don't misunderstand," Torigoe added. "I'm simply not that expressive."

"See?" I told Fushimi, who was still using me as a shield.

She kept squirming behind me, so I pushed her in front of Torigoe.

"Torigoe didn't object to your idea because she hates you. Right?"

"He's right. I wasn't even that against the idea."

It's normal to feel like a rejection of your idea is a rejection of you, but Torigoe wasn't the kind of person to actually oppose someone that way.

"Torigoe… I just… I just thought we could all have fun this way…"

"Stop."

"Huh?"

"I'm calling you Hiina now, so you should stop calling me Torigoe."

"Then what do I call you?"

"You could call me Shii, like Mii does. Or Shizu, like his sis does."

"Then…Shii," she timidly said.

Torigoe nodded. "Good."

The darkness was slowly lifting from Fushimi's expression.

I looked at Torigoe's hands and the book underneath them, and I burst out laughing when I saw the title.

"After all that, Torigoe, you're still up for it, aren't you?"

It was *The Beginner's Guide to Screenwriting*.

"Ah…" She immediately hid it behind her back.

"…No, this…just got returned; I was about to put it back…" Her face was getting red. "B-besides, it's not like the class already accepted Hiina's idea…"

"I think you're fit for the job, Torigoe. If it does end up happening. You've got a lot of experience reading novels, and if anyone else says they want to do it, you can just work together."

Fushimi nodded as hard as she could. "Good…to hear…"

"Looking forward to seeing your work, Miss Writer. If it does happen."

They shared a handshake, and all was well that ended well.

"Ryou, whatcha thiiink?" Fushimi said in a weirdly funny voice, staring at me with a smirk on our way home from the station.

"About what? The career survey?"

"No… Stop acting like you don't know what I mean."

Torigoe had accepted her assignment as the screenwriter for her film. Now she was waiting for my decision.

"Director, eh… I don't know what a director does, though…"

"Direct everyone, of course."

"I think there's someone better for that role right in front of me now."

"Huh? Me?"

"Yes. I'm sure you've watched more movies than I have, and you probably have an idea of how you want it shot."

"Well…maybe, yeah."

The main actor was also in the director's seat. It'd be like someone in baseball being both the ace pitcher and cleanup hitter.

"Surely there has to be someone else in class better for the job than me, right?"

"There isn't."

No room for doubt? Why?

"I want you to do it."

"That's not an argument…"

Don't be so childish.

"We still have to decide the story's themes, but I want to do it right. I don't want it to be crappy."

That's gonna take a lot of preparation… We need the tools, props, a place to shoot it…

That was also why she suggested it as a solution for *"Everyone can do their part."*

"We haven't even decided to do it yet."

"But you already know how it went last meeting… The problem is that no one's suggesting what to do anymore. This one made it through everyone's prohibitions, so they'll agree!"

We reached her house before I knew it.

"Think about it! Actually, just get ready to say yes!" She giggled, then waved good-bye as she went inside.

We started getting back our midterms results, and I got better grades than expected.

"See, Ryou? I knew you could do it with a little effort." Fushimi seemed happier about it than I was.

I even managed to avoid failing English.

"Well done. Now you don't have to come to supplementary classes," Waka said when giving me back my test result of forty-eight. "Keep it up."

"Thanks."

She didn't say anything about my career survey. Was she saving that for later? Or did she forget?

We reported our progress regarding the school festival's previous meeting, but Waka simply scratched her head. "Yeah, I realize it's hard to come to an agreement. Anyway, let's keep it going in our next long homeroom. I'll leave you to take the lead again, class reps."

Now the day's last long homeroom was here, and Waka was nowhere to be found.

"The teacher told us to keep talking about our plans for the school festival," Fushimi said, walking up to the front. I followed and wrote down on the blackboard the list of things no one wanted to do. "So now, let's talk about what we *do* want to do. Anyone have any ideas?"

As expected, we had zero takers. Just a big list of nos.

Fushimi cleared her throat. "Well then, I have a suggestion myself." Everyone paid close attention to what she would say next. "How about we make an indie film? No one mentioned this on the list of things they don't want, right?"

She turned to me for confirmation.

"Nope, as you can see, no one shot down anything that specific."

The reactions came next.

"A film, huh?"

"We'd just have to show it the day of, so that sounds nice."

"Oh man, what if I have to play the lead?"

"Don't worry—that's never gonna happen."

It got everyone talking, in a good way. Most reactions were positive.

Fushimi went back to her seat and pulled out a plastic sleeve full of papers from her desk.

Did she actually do it? Did she prepare a proposal document?

"Pass these to those behind you." She handed out copies for everyone, then gave one to me last. "Here, Ryou."

"Okay."

It was a list of pros and cons about making a film.

"As you can see, if we decide on this project, we would only need a few people to stay here during the festival to manage the showing, while the others can go hang out elsewhere. We'd be taking turns, obviously. You can look around with your boyfriend or girlfriend, eat at the places other classes are putting on, or whatever else you want."

The downside was that we would need to take a lot of time beforehand to actually make it. However, we wouldn't need to work long hours—we could make it little by little.

"And the greatest thing about this is that it won't just stay in our memories—we'd get to keep the results forever."

You had to eventually take down whatever else you did: haunted mansion, café, etc. On the other hand, we could keep the movie as long as we wanted.

Everyone listened attentively to Fushimi's presentation.

"And since it will stay with us forever, I want to make it the best that we can."

I could tell people were feeling moved by her passion. She'd even taken the care to prepare this whole presentation, and the document also made it clear she was thinking about how everyone could do their part. There was a list of necessary duties on the other side of the paper: a minimum number of people that added up to the exact amount in our class.

"What do you think?"

After a short silence, one girl spoke up. "This idea sounds good, Hina."

"Yeah, it might be nice having everyone come together like this for once."

"Now this is what I call youth."

"We are in second year of high school! Doesn't get better than this!"

"…Let's go for it, then."

Fushimi beamed and turned to look at me. I awkwardly smiled back at her.

"So what's it gonna be about, then?" one of the boys said; then people started throwing out ideas while I wrote them down.

A war drama set in space, excellent… You guys are actually insane. I wrote it down anyway.

"Um, we only have a budget of fifty thousand yen… Though if Waka feels like it, she might give us up to thirty thousand out of her pocket."

We have a budget? I didn't know that. Waka only ever tells these things to Fushimi. Good judgment, I must admit.

"Waka's gonna give us thirty thousand yen?!"

"Wait, hold on! Only if she feels like it, okay?"

All hail Waka's magnanimity.

"Is there anyone who can help come up with the story of the film? So concept planning and screenwriting. We have Torigoe at the helm for now…" Torigoe jumped up, startled, then froze at hearing her name. "We just have to be mindful of the content; making anything too intense could be hard…"

"Torigoe, the silent beauty…? I guess she is always reading books."

She wasn't that silent, actually, but I guessed our classmates rarely ever talked with her.

Writing a screenplay had to be different from a novel, but it seemed there was no one else as deeply engaged in storytelling as she was. Most people occasionally watched movies or anime or read manga…including me, honestly, but actually making one was a whole other thing. No one was volunteering to help her out.

Then one of the boys spoke up on behalf of the rest. "I want to entrust this to SB Torigoe."

Is that supposed to be an abbreviation for Silent Beauty? Come on.

"Okay then, Shii will be our screenwriter."

Torigoe ducked her head from embarrassment, hearing her nickname out of nowhere.

"Shii?"

"Is that supposed to be Torigoe?"

"Oh, like *shhh*? Because she's silent?"

"That makes sense."

The misunderstandings only made Torigoe's face turn redder and redder.

Fushimi asked me to start taking notes, so I erased what was already there and wrote down: **Screenplay: SB Torigoe.**

"Side back…?" a member of the soccer club muttered.

"About the leading role…" I spoke up on my own for the first time in this meeting. "I think Fushimi should be it."

My childhood friend turned toward me, startled. Might be better if she didn't nominate herself.

"I don't mind, but…," one of the girls said as she and her neighbors looked at one another in confusion. "We haven't even decided what to do. Is there any point in choosing a main actor now?"

"We can't do anything too complicated, since we have a limited budget. Also, considering the costs of costumes and such, I think the most realistic choice would be to have a high school student as the protagonist."

Half of them seemed to agree with my point, but the other half still wasn't persuaded.

"Well, we're all in high school, aren't we? So that means any of us could be it."

I glanced at Fushimi. She hesitated for a bit, frown on her face, and then nodded.

Okay, that's it. Let's go for broke.

"Fushimi is studying to become an actress. I think she's better fit for the job than anyone else in class."

"Huh?" "Seriously?" "Fushimi's becoming an actress?" "Wow!" A small stir was rising in the room.

I spoke up again before it could gain too much momentum. "Besides"—*and this is the important part*—"is there anyone else who could get us a bigger audience than her?"

"Yeah, people will probably come if we advertise it."

"At least her friends and other people interested in her would come."

"Then…"

"None of you imagined an empty theater or a tiny audience when you heard about us showing the film, right?"

No one watched a movie more than once unless they loved it. And what hope would we have as amateurs? Most likely it'd be kinda boring.

"As you can see, Fushimi is quite pretty."

"S-stop it, Ryou!" she yelped in a panic, her face beet red.

"I don't think there's anyone better for it, in both skills and advertising."

I didn't realize at first how serious Fushimi was about this. She had never been this proactive in all my years of being her classmate. So I figured I'd end up on the sidelines again, going through the motions to get this festival over and done with, but that wasn't the case. I didn't imagine she'd be that assertive—it went to show just how much she wanted to make this movie and how much she wanted to be the leading actor. And I wanted to help her achieve that. She would make it worth our time.

"I want the most people to see the fruits of our efforts."

That clinched it. No one objected anymore; now we only needed to hear her thoughts.

"Geez, Ryou... I didn't expect you to call me p-pretty." She was turning bright red, completely forgetting she was in front of the class.

"Stop with the blushing. Now what do you say? Will you do it?"

"...I will," she said toward me. I pointed at the rest of the class with my chin.

I already know you will. You have to say it to them.

"I... I've been studying a bit of acting, and I even had the opportunity to perform once, so I do think I probably know more about this than anyone else here. So please, let me do it." She bowed; then applause roared.

"Yeah. Plus, who wants more arguments trying to find someone else who would be willing to do it?"

"That's true. We have plenty of other decisions to make, so no time for that."

"Us guys would probably put all our votes on the princess."

Fushimi's eyes met mine, and then she smiled. "Thanks, Ryou."

"No problem. I just figured people would be weirded out or push back if you said it yourself. Guess I was right to jump in front of you."

Everyone knew criticizing her would invite a mob of her fans, so I worried that if anyone was against it, they wouldn't feel safe speaking up.

Then the bell rang, and everyone left their seats.

I started writing down today's summary in my notebook when Fushimi asked, "R-Ryou, d-did you really mean that?"

"Huh? What?"

"You know, that..." She hesitated, then whispered, "That I'm pretty..."

"It's not a matter of personal taste. That's just fact."

"Geeeez!" She hit my shoulder. "You should just... Gosh, why...?" She sighed heavily.

"Hiina. Congrats on the role."

"Yeah, thanks."

"Now please stop flirting in the classroom."

"I'm most certainly not," I replied while keeping my eyes on the notebook.

"Are you mad I'm the one he called pretty, Shii?"

The hell?

I looked up, surprised by Fushimi's strange reaction. I could see a dark aura behind her smile.

"I'm just telling you to do your jobs instead of playing around," Torigoe replied with a smile.

...What is happening in here?

It felt like playing with fire in a gunpowder factory.

"You know, I was thinking about writing a story with a male protagonist."

"Oh, that's perfectly fine. I can play a man, too."

"...Yeah, it doesn't seem like you'd have any trouble with that chest."

Torigoe. Please. Dear Torigoe. Don't take the fire so close to the fuse.

"That has nothing to do with what I'm saying! I just said that I have the acting skills for the job!"

Hold on, please.

"C'mon—we just finished the meeting on a positive note! Stop arguing."

""I'm not arguing.""

How are you in such perfect sync?

"Back on topic, how long should we make it?"

"One hour? I guess that might be too long—how about around thirty minutes?"

Now they're talking like nothing happened... I really don't get women.

"Let's say we have three showings: one in the morning, one in the afternoon, one in the evening..."

Torigoe and Fushimi then started passionately talking about what kind of movie *theater* we'd be using, rather than the film itself. I tried chiming in—"Does it matter?"—but their glares scared me into silence for the rest of the conversation. Good judgment on my part.

We took the class journal to the staff room, and their discussion was still going on when we were exiting the school building. They talked about movies, then changed to the books they were based off, then started talking about how amazing this or that book would be as a movie. The train kept on going and showed no sign of stopping, and I was outside the circle all the while.

Maybe I'll start watching more movies and reading more books...

I really did feel left out now.

"I want to talk about our film with Takamori, so can I go home with you?"

Fushimi formed an X with her arms. "Nope. You can't." She left no room for discussion.

"C'mon! It's just this one time. It's not fair only you get to do it, Hiina."

"Okay, I guess I can allow it. Once."

"Wait a second, what about my opinion?"

Your house isn't even in this direction, is it, Torigoe?

Once we reached the point where we had to go our separate ways, Torigoe left us with some sadness.

Fushimi and I crossed the ticket gates and got on the train. Seats were open, so we sat down, and I finally got to catch my breath. Fushimi then started tapping my sneakers with her loafers.

"What?"

"Nothing." She giggled. "Ryou...you love me, don't you?"

My heart almost jumped out of my chest.

"Why?!"

"How else would you be able to say that in public? I know you do." She looked at me with absolute confidence, then wrapped her arms around mine.

"There's no doubt in my mind. And actually, hearing you say that just makes me love you even more…"

…

"A-as I said, I was literally being completely objective…"

"Then tell me what you think, subjectively." She pouted.

I could almost get lost in her shapely face and adorable mannerisms. I had to look away.

"O-one day."

"Hee-hee. You're blushing."

"No, I'm not," I said. The most obvious lie ever.

©Fly

We left the station, walking our way home.

"I'm glad everything went well during the meeting."

"Yup. Though there's still one very important role that hasn't been officially decided yet. Remember?" she asked, looking me right in the eye. "Is there even anyone who could do it but you? Do you have any ideas?"

"Well… I'm sure someone will want to give it a try if we ask."

Fushimi groaned, then said with a firm tone, "I'll just 'fess up. I want to make this with you and Shii, not anyone else. It'll be my first school festival with you!"

"That's not true. We've been in the same class forever."

"I mean, yeah, but you never participated in this stuff. Neither did I."

Fair point.

"But that has nothing to do with me being director—"

Fushimi interrupted me. "Look, we're all amateurs here. Even me—I barely have any experience. Same for Shii's screenwriting. Everyone will be making a film for the first time in their lives."

"But I'm not sure I can do it—"

"It doesn't matter!" Her voice echoed throughout the quiet neighborhood.

"You could end up regretting not doing it later! You should just take the chance! It doesn't matter if you can't do it right!"

"Wait, doesn't that go against what you said in the classroom?"

*   *   *

I didn't want to fail. I didn't want to embarrass myself. What was the point if I couldn't do it right? Besides, I could already imagine what would happen if I—someone with barely any friends—messed it up. They'd all turn on me. I tried to convince myself I didn't care about such criticism, but I couldn't fool myself. I was scared.

"None of us really knows what we're doing, so no one will pin the blame on you. It's not like we're going to get dogpiled on the Internet, either."

Things won't go right. That was the only reason I needed to not put effort into something. I was scared of actually trying hard.

"What? Hold on. You said you wanted to make something good, didn't you?"

"I did. And I'm sure we can do it with you at the helm."

"How can you even know that? Where do you get that confidence?!"

"I know it! I saw it today, during that meeting!"

"I'm not like you. Real life never goes the way I want. You're like a protagonist; I'm not."

I was sure my childhood friend would become a successful actress. She had the looks, the passion, and was putting in the effort. And so she'd become less and less like the girl I knew...

"...'Protagonist'? What the hell? That's ridiculous. Have you always seen me that way?" Her eyes were suddenly welling up. I wondered why, but I said nothing. "Ryou, treat me like I'm normal. Don't put me on a pedestal like everyone else!"

I took a moment to think of what to say. "...I'm sorry," I finally apologized. "But I don't know what to do. I don't have my future laid out for me. But you—"

You'll become an actress, just like you want.

"I don't know! I don't!" She cut me off. "Nothing's set in stone! I'm just a beginner. I've got nothing but dreams right now. But I really do love doing it!" Fushimi wasn't holding anything back. "I knew I could run away if I didn't say anything. I could just find an excuse and give up. But I didn't want you to think of me as a quitter, so I needed the courage to tell you…"

So that's why she said that…

"Wait! Please give me some time before I can tell you that. Sorry."

"I, um… I need to prepare myself for it."

"I have my own issues, too, you know?! I worry about how I'm getting along with my friends; I worry about what the future might be like; I worry about our relationship! I'm a normal girl! I'm not special! I'm not a 'protagonist'! Stop saying that!"

Fushimi finally took a breath after letting it all out.

She was no stranger. She was still the Fushimi I knew.

"So you have worries, too."

"Of course. And also…" She squinted grumpily. "Why didn't you say anything when I showed you my career survey saying *actress* for all three options?! You should've been mad that I told you we'd go to college together!"

"You said it was 'another story'…"

That it wasn't that unusual to work while you're in college.

She pinched my cheek.

"Hey, stop! Why do you do that?"

"I'm not talking about the logic! I'm talking about your feelings!"

What?

"I wanted you to tell me to give up on being an actress to be by your side!"

"I'm not saying that. I support you."

"Ugggh. I kinda have mixed feelings, but… Well, I'm glad!"

Good to hear.

"It's fine if you don't know what career path to take. It's fine if you don't know what you want to do. You do you, Ryou."

©Fly

"Yeah, that's the part I don't really get…"

"The one thing I have noticed is that you seemed to have fun editing that video for Mana and taking my video. You couldn't see your face, but you were really into it."

I had no idea. I only did it because I didn't *hate* it, but was I really enjoying it that much?

"I think you're just bad at noticing how you feel."

Mana said the same exact thing.

"I'll teach you! I'll show you what it is to feel happy, to feel fun, to feel in love! I'll guide you through everything! You'll see I'm not like other girls!"

Didn't you just say not to treat you like you're special? But the inconsistency had me smiling.

She was happy, determined, full of confidence. This was her stage, and she wouldn't share it with anyone.

"Don't worry. I'll be by your side."

I didn't want to try because I was scared of failure, and so I never succeeded… I was scared that I'd never amount to anything.

"You said you weren't a protagonist, right? Then let me say: This protagonist wants you. It's fine if you don't know; it's fine if you can't see your future. Still—because of it, I want to go on with you. Let's do this together, Ryou!"

For some reason, my eyes were starting to sting. Fushimi pulled me close and wrapped an arm around my head.

"Oh, got any news?"

It was Friday morning. I went to the staff room, and Waka stopped typing on her computer when she saw me.

"News?"

"About the school festival. You didn't report any progress yesterday."

"Oh, right." I forgot, since she didn't ask. "Um, here's how it's going."

I showed her my notes summarizing what we'd talked about then.

Waka nodded. "Sounds good. A film, huh? Could be cheaper than a haunted house." She chuckled.

"We still don't have any concrete story ideas, though... What's with that face?"

She was glancing at me, then back at the notebook, then back at me with a smirk.

"Do your best, director."

"...Ah... Yeah."

"What does the director do, by the way?"

"I'm still not really sure."

We chatted for a bit; then she looked up at me with a smile.

"I thought you were the apathetic type, but it seems I was wrong."

"I just thought I'd give it a shot."

"Oh, don't try to play dumb. Ah, are you playing games? Are you about to finally go soft and sweet on me?"

Not on your life, so don't worry about that possibility.

"Oh, also this. I still hadn't submitted it." I took out the piece of paper from my bag.

"Right, that. The career survey. I was thinking about telling you. Good thing you mentioned it yourself."

I gave her my career survey, only one thing written on it. Waka burst out laughing when she saw it. "Ha-ha-ha. Good. Making the most of your youth."

"There's no need to laugh."

"It's actually refreshing." Waka checked my name off the list. "That's all of them! 'I don't know,' huh? Ha-ha-ha. Honest. This one's gonna be a doozy during the parent-teacher meeting!"

"Stop laughing."

"Sorry, sorry."

Why does she seem like she's looking forward to that meeting?

"My mom's pretty forgiving on stuff like that, so I don't think there'll be a problem."

"Oh, really?" Her eyebrows rose.

My work was done, so I left the staff room. Fushimi was waiting for me outside.

"So what did you write for the survey, Ryou?"

"It's a secret."

"Whaaat? I wanna know!"

I started down the hallway, and she stuck by my side

"Anyway, can't wait for our film festival tomorrow!" she said with excitement.

She was planning on taking as many DVDs as she could to my house.

"I can't watch too many at a time," I replied.

"Just my favorites, then."

"Fine, fine."

Well, we'd take this one step at a time.

We were having lunch in the physics room, chatting about a movie we'd all happened to see on TV a few days before.

"They're always showing it, but that was the first time I'd actually seen it."

It was, like, ultra-famous.

"It was the second time for me. What did you think about it, Takamori?" asked Torigoe.

"It was fun. I can see why so many people like it."

"Me too. I'd forgotten a decent chunk of it, so I still enjoyed it."

Fushimi then slowly shook her head, this know-it-all look on her face. "The director's work back then still had this edge to it. Nowadays, it's all so mainstream pandering. I mean, I still like the movies, but they feel different." She sighed.

"Hiina's weirdly pedantic, don't you think, Takamori?"

"Hey, you didn't have to say that. And don't expect me to back you up."

Fushimi didn't seem to have heard her; she kept on looking at us mainstream plebs from her high horse.

"Ryou, Ryou, if you liked that one, I have another that's even better. I'll lend you the DVD."

"I don't really want to watch deeper movies. I'm fine with mainstream. Let's just keep it to the popular ones I still haven't seen."

"Whaaat?" She was very upset.

"Yeah, I know her type." Torigoe was adding insult to injury. "People who think things were always better back in the day and that popular stuff is somehow bad. Didn't know you were one of *those*, Hiina."

"That's not what I meant!"

"You literally just said that."

I could only look back and forth, watching the virtual tennis match.

"You said the same thing but about novels, didn't you, Shii?"

"I did? No way." Torigoe waved her hand in disbelief. "I never said things were better back in the day, just that we can learn from the past. Old things can also be good."

"Yes, yes, exactly! I said just the same thing."

"But you also criticized the director for starting to pander to the mainstream."

"I'm just saying that I liked the edge of his older films, and I miss it in his more recent work. I'm not saying I hate all mainstream movies." Fushimi seemed pretty excited to debate this, all things considered; maybe she never got to do it with anyone else.

"I get what you're feeling, but..." Torigoe, too, seemed to grow more talkative.

"You two sure get along," I commented.

They didn't hear my comment, though, and immediately started listing their top five novels and top five films.

"See, Shii? All you like are the classics."

"You too, Hiina. It's like you just listed top black-and-white films. What age were you even born in?"

"Ugh."

"..."

Fushimi puffed out her cheeks, while Torigoe looked away.

...Do *they get along?*

Then I remembered one thing Fushimi had said she liked that wasn't on her list.

"Fushimi, didn't you say you like this romantic flick based on a girls' manga?"

"Agh!" Fushimi buried her head in her hands.

Torigoe chuckled. "I thought you'd make fun of that kind of thing."

"Oh, and Torigoe, you said you liked this romantic-comedy harem light novel, right?"

"…No, I'm just…branching out, you know?"

"Ohhhh? I never would've guessed." Fushimi started giggling as well.

"There you go—that's a draw." I put an end to their argument, since it seemed like it could go on forever.

I told Mana about it once I got home, and she snorted.

"I mean, sure, it's fine to criticize it if it's boring or whatever. But who cares as long as you enjoy it?" She tilted her head, puzzled.

Mana, Bubby thinks you win this argument.

Everyone was staring at the hanging strap they were holding on to or at the ads posted on the windows, their lifeless faces like a bunch of robots.

I couldn't freely chat with Fushimi when there were so many people on the train.

The PA repeated the name of the station where we'd arrived, and people poured out of the doors. But they were immediately replaced.

"Byuh…" Fushimi let out a strange squeal as we got separated by the crowd. I could see her hand reaching to me, but soon enough, it disappeared into the sea of people.

Will she be okay?

She had said she'd gotten used to the packed trains after a while of riding with me, but she still sometimes disappeared like this.

She'd proposed biking to school together, but I rejected the idea because it was always either too hot or too cold, depending on the day, but maybe it was time to reconsider. I got worried whenever she disappeared into the crowd, considering she had almost been molested before.

I tried to see where she'd disappeared to and spotted a high school girl nearby wearing a uniform I didn't recognize. She must've gotten on the train at the last stop. I doubted her school was around these parts; in fact, our school was the only one in this direction.

Behind her was a salaryman who looked to be in his fifties. Not good. Her face started turning pale, her hands gripping the strap hard. I could tell the dude was taking advantage of the train's swaying to get his face unnaturally close.

"Excuse me…" I forced myself in between the two, receiving a look of annoyance and angry mumbling.

My back was to her, and my eyes met the old guy's at point-blank range. There was an uncomfortably intense look in them that I didn't like. It also felt like the swaying of the train could force us to kiss if I wasn't careful. I pursed my lips and looked away. Then he stomped my foot with full force.

You bastard!

We arrived at the next station, and someone grabbed my wrist.

Huh? What?

They pulled me away from the old guy. I turned to see who was grabbing my wrist and saw it was the girl I was (trying to) defend. She dragged me all the way out of the train before letting me go.

"This guy's a molester!"

Wait, wait, wait!

"Hold on! No, I'm not! In fact, I was just trying to help…"

Everyone around was looking at us. The doors of the train closed, and as it went away, I could see Fushimi saying something through the window.

"I was trying to protect you from that guy behind…"

"He was whispering into my ear about how good I smell…"

We defended ourselves until, finally, we were able to see each other's faces.

Huh? Have I met her before…?

"What? No way. Are you…Ryou?"

There was only one person who called me that.

"Ai…?"

Ai Himejima. The girl who had transferred schools back in elementary. My other childhood friend.

Afterword

Hello, I'm Kennoji.

The first volume of the series managed to get a reprint immediately, thanks to the reception, and now here is the second entry.

We finally got to see Shino, the character teased at the end of the previous volume. What did you think? I never went through this myself, but I believe that sort of experience the protagonist had is pretty common in middle school. Granted, I never heard of someone lasting only three days, but I think it's a very fitting end for the edgy middle schooler Shinohara.

We also see the main character's Unique Skill in action for this event: Obliviousness. Seriously, I wished he'd get a clue already, too, even though I'm the writer. I think this comes from the train of thought people with low self-esteem usually have: *Of course no one would actually be interested in me*. So it takes a while to realize that such feelings are being directed at you. That's the kind of main character we have for this story.

The Skill's absolute power might be having you feel bad for the heroines, but I hope you can keep on reading with warm hope.

We also have a new heroine at the end of this volume, so please look forward to the next.

Many people helped make possible this second volume, so I would like to thank them. I want to give special thanks to Fly for continuing to provide the illustrations, despite their busy schedule. Thank you very much for the beautiful pictures of Fushimi and the other heroines in this volume. I hope we can keep working together for much longer.

I also want to thank my editor in charge, the designer for the book, everyone in sales, proofreading, the bookstore clerks, and each and every one of you involved in the production and sale of this book.

And finally, I want to thank you, the reader. And if you are reading this before deciding to buy it, please go ahead and take it to the register!

Look forward to the third volume!

KENNOJI